MURDER OF A BOOKSELLER

When bookseller Brian McDonald is murdered — stabbed in the back with his own paperknife — the police are overwhelmed with suspects! Investigating detective Bentley Hollow discovers that the victim, dishonest professionally and privately, was universally hated by those closest to him. For the detective, life is difficult, his wife has left him and there's a mutual hatred between him and his police partner. Now, in finding the murderer *and* a solution to his problems, his life would be irrevocably changed . . .

Books by Gary Lovisi
in the Linford Mystery Library:

GARY LOVISI

---◆---

MURDER OF A BOOKSELLER

Complete and Unabridged

LINFORD
Leicester

First published in Great Britain

First Linford Edition
published 2012

British Library CIP Data

Lovisi, Gary.
   Murder of a bookseller.- -
   (Linford mystery library)
   1. Detective and mystery stories.
   2. Large type books.
   I. Title II. Series
   813.6–dc23

   ISBN 978–1–4448–0998–5

Published by
F. A. Thorpe (Publishing)
Anstey, Leicestershire

Set by Words & Graphics Ltd.
Anstey, Leicestershire
Printed and bound in Great Britain by
T. J. International Ltd., Padstow, Cornwall

This book is printed on acid-free paper

Part 1

Death of a Bookseller

Prologue:

'I'm surprised to see you,' Brian McDonald said cautiously, allowing the visitor to enter his home. 'You know I sell books, but it is by appointment only.'

'I remember, but I must have that book, not just a copy or a reprint, I want the original and I want it right away.'

'Really? Well, I'm just surprised, that is all. You know it's pricey. So you like Jim Thompson?'

'I like him — his work, I mean. But mainly I want it because it is a book that my father had in his collection years ago. It was one of his favourites. So, I want it back now.'

'Well, that's nice, I'm sure. Do you have the money?'

'Of course.'

'Then come in. Let's go upstairs to my office.'

'You have the book here?'

'Of course. *Now and on Earth* by Jim

Thompson, Modern Age, 1942, the first edition in hardcover and jacket of the author's first book. Near fine in a near fine dust jacket. A prize piece, a cornerstone for any serious Thompson collector, or collector of noir and hardboiled crime. So you collect Thompson?'

'In my own way.'

McDonald shrugged, 'Well, I want $25,000 for it. Do you have the cash with you?'

'Yes, but that is much too much, I'm sure you'll take a flat $20,000 cash.'

'No, I don't think so. As I told you, $25,000 is my firm price.'

'No, I think you will see it my way, for old time's sake. I can give you $20,000 cash right now. I have 200, one-hundred dollar bills. See?'

McDonald was silent looking at the cash being held up in front of his face. It was a big, fat pile of hundreds. Was his mouth actually watering?

'I told you, $25,000 is my firm price.'

'Well, then I will walk, and you get nothing.'

'Wait! Okay, okay, $20,000. You're

getting a very good deal.'

'Sure.'

'Come into my office. You can place the money on my desk. Here is the book. Look it over. You like it?'

'Yes and I'll take it.'

'Good,' McDonald replied and he pocketed the cash quickly. Then he took out a thick binder and opened it to the section beginning with 'T' and began thumbing through it. He looked up at his visitor for just a second and explained, 'I just have to write the sale here in my book and take it off my list, then we will be done.'

'Sure, I'll wait while you finish up.'

'I'll just be a minute,' Brian McDonald said, now sitting at his desk with the opened book in front of him, his head buried in the record book busy filling in the date and terms of sale.

His customer stood behind him watching patiently.

The bookseller's full attention was now on the wad of cash in his pocket and in looking up the sale in the book in front of him.

5

'There's just one more thing.'

'Eh?' McDonald asked absently.

'*This!*'

The silver letter opener that had moments before lain innocently upon the desk was plunged full-force into the top of Brian McDonald's back. It went in deep and hard with a force and rage unexpected, down into the man's spine, scraping bone. There was remarkably little blood.

McDonald shook, froze, looked up into the face of his killer and then died instantly. His head fell down onto the desk, but the sales book was not there any longer. The murderer was holding the book now, while the gleaming silver letter opener stuck out of the bookseller's back like a shiny beacon of death.

Next the killer took back the cash and cleaned off McDonald's desk of all papers, throwing them to the floor carelessly, picking up a thick black marker to write an angry message in bold, fiery block letters upon the desktop.

1

Uneasy Partners

'Hollow!' I heard the harsh voice of Captain Wallace bark from his corner office. 'Hollow! Grant! Get in here now!'

I looked up from my desk in the squad room and straight into the face of the man sitting directly opposite me. That man was Detective Charlie Grant, a guy I hated almost as much as he hated me.

Most detective partners had desks in the squad room placed flush front to front, facing each other, so each detective would always be able to see the mug of their closest cop buddy when he looked up from his desk. Until recently, that had been my long-time partner, Don Evans. He was a great guy who had just retired, so I was now flying solo. Charlie Grant's partner, Ed Morgan, had recently died from a massive and sudden heart attack. So Grant and I were both flying solo now.

We both knew that couldn't last.

Yesterday, Captain Wallace moved Grant across from me into Don's old desk. I took that as an omen of things to come. A bad omen.

Charlie Grant looked up at me, shook his head, 'The old man's on a tear, we'd better get in there fast.'

I shrugged, I didn't care about the old man or his problems, I had my own problems to worry about. My wife, Beth, had recently left me for a swanky doctor across town. She'd cleaned out our bank account, and she'd even taken some of the best pieces of Depression Glass that we'd collected over the years. Some of that stuff was now worth a good bit of cash. She'd taken the quality items and had left me with a quantity of second-rate stuff. I was lucky to have that left. I didn't know which was worse, losing the wife — who had become a marginal friend and less-than-marginal lover over the last few years anyway — or losing all that valuable collectable glassware. Being a collector myself, I figured it was a toss up.

'I'll take my time, if you don't mind,' I

told the guy across from me. I didn't even want to think of him as my partner yet. So far he wasn't, and I hoped that would last for a while longer. 'We're not dogs that jump to our master's voice.'

'*Hollow! Grant!* Get the hell in here *now!*' the old man barked out again. It was loud and full of menace.

Grant and I jumped then, right out of our seats and hurried into the Captain's small glass-enclosed office at the back of the squad room. Grant closed the door behind him softly.

Captain Tyler Wallace was an ornery old coot at the best of times who was a charter member of the KMA Club — kiss my ass — he being a few years past the retirement age where he was on schedule to get a good pension. He didn't give a damn about much and didn't care who knew it. He was seated behind his desk, which he used like a battleship to bully, intimidate and scare the hell out of rookies, and even some old coppers. This morning his face was twisted with concern and worry. 'Don't sit down, gentlemen, you won't be here that long.'

I looked at Grant and then back to the Captain, hoping and praying that he wasn't going to do what I thought he might do — that is, team Grant and I up on a case.

'Grant, Hollow, I'm going to team you up on this case,' Wallace said slowly, allowing his words to sink in. My heart sank. I hated Grant, and he hated me. We had our reasons. 'Grant, you're my best detective, and Hollow, you . . . I hear you collect a lot of old crap, like antiques and stuff, glass and other junk like old books. Well, don't you?

'A little,' I ventured carefully. The way Captain Wallace described me, it sounded like I was the local junk man, but I only collected Depression glassware, and not much of that. Only select pieces, and at select prices that I could afford. But I was a collector and I did understand the mentality, so maybe he was right, in his own twisted, over-simplified way of thinking, to pick me for a case that involved collectors.

'Great! That's just what I need, someone who understands these freaks that collect all this old crap. Books in this case.' he said, shaking his head, like it was a mystery why anyone would want to collect books of all things — much less read them!

'I'm not a book collector, Captain,' I corrected him, just to set the record straight. 'I don't know books at all.'

'You'll learn. Doesn't matter really, you collect old stuff, so you get the idea,' he looked at me sternly. Some reaction by me was called for.

I nodded.

'Good, then it's settled. We just got a call from 101 Montrose, home of Brian McDonald. The man is some kind of rare book dealer. The guy was murdered late last night, by all accounts, stabbed in the back. The body is still fresh, uniforms are there now, lab boys on the way. Get there fast and close this case.'

We both nodded, got set to leave. Neither of us was happy.

'Now listen,' Wallace added in a sharp but low tone, 'there's something else. I just got a follow-up call from the first uniform on the scene. He found

McDonald dead but he also found something scribbled on the man's desk by his body, it was some kind of message. Now keep this quiet. I don't know if it is a part of this investigation or not, but we can't ignore it. I just want you to keep it quiet.'

'What's the message, Captain?' Charlie Grant asked suspiciously, he had taken out a piece of Juicy Fruit gum and was chewing away happily, like he didn't have a care in the world. If you knew Grant, that's the way he was.

'Book Collectors, Go To Hell!'

'Book Collectors . . . ?' I stammered.

'Damn!' Grant replied, not chewing any longer.

'Get on it, guys — and you, Hollow, I want to see something from you on this — and not in the papers. Now both of you, get out!'

★ ★ ★

The house at 101 Montrose was a four bedroom Tudor in an upscale part of town that oozed money and class. Grant and I walked through the yellow crime scene tape and passed the cop on duty at the front door, who let us in after we flashed him our badges.

'All right, Hollow, I'll take the lead on this one. We'll clear it up quicker that way,' Grant said with his characteristic bravado and annoying arrogance. 'I'll show you how it's done.'

'Gee, thanks,' I replied sarcastically. Then I couldn't resist adding, 'Yeah, that's rich, you'll show me?'

He suddenly stopped walking, his gaze searching my face. 'You're not going to give me any trouble on this, are you, boy?'

Boy? I guess I was 'boy' now because I was younger than he was. Or maybe not as experienced — like not experienced in taking money, doctoring evidence, framing up perps to get a case closed. That kind of experience that I knew was par for the course for cops like Grant. I remembered now all the reasons that I didn't like Charlie Grant and realized I'd have to keep an eye on him.

'Take the lead, I don't care,' I said pulling back, trying to diffuse any argument, at least for the moment. I mean, we hadn't even entered the murder house yet — and it seemed already things were getting hot between us.

'That's better,' Grant told me as he walked inside the house. I shook my head as I followed him, but the blockhead just couldn't leave it all there, he couldn't resist taking another stab at my apparent weakness being intimidated by his bully words. I wasn't, but I didn't want any trouble.

It got me hot when he added, 'Good to see you know your place, Hollow.'

Well, that did it for me. My hand flew to his shoulder and I pulled him backwards, twisting him around so we faced each other. I pushed him hard against the wall of the narrow foyer, my face a bare inch from his own. I could see the sweat gleaming on his face now, the fear in his little pig eyes. Grant was just your garden-variety bully, after all. Maybe I was too, because no sooner had I braced him than I realized I had made a terrible mistake. It was so stupid but I couldn't stop myself. I really disliked this guy.

I'd totally lost control and barked into his face, 'Listen, numbnuts, the old man says we gotta work this case together, so that means *together!* You screw around with me and I'll do you double back. Got it?'

I pushed him away from me with disgust and he lost his balance, wobbled into the wall, straightened himself, then glared at me insanely for a long tense moment. Suddenly he smiled at me. It was weird. I had to admit that his smile was even more unnerving than his usual anger and mad glare. Was I wrong about Grant? Maybe he was more dangerous than I had first thought?

'You stay away from me, Hollow, you got that!' Grant barked in a low tone filled with the promise of menace to come. 'You ever do that again and I'll fix you up, fix you up good!'

'You threatening me?' I said, ready to check him hard if he made a lunge at me.

I saw him pat the weapon in the holster under his arm, 'Come on. Try me, just try me, asshole!'

I backed off, the situation between us

was a lot worse than I ever expected and a lot worse than I needed to deal with while beginning a new case. I'd been so stupid, getting hot about his words. I knew a lot of it had been my fault, my anger at his insults, but I just couldn't keep on holding back. I knew I'd have to cool down, otherwise I'd blow the entire case. Probably my career, as well.

'Look,' I told him, trying for a more conciliatory manner, 'we got a murder here, so let's just solve it and get this done. Then that'll be the end of it, and of us.'

'You put your hands on me, Hollow. I don't forget that.'

'Fine. Look, I admit I was out of line, but you provoked me for no reason. If you want to brood about it, brood about it all you want. We still have a job to do. Now, you want to go upstairs and check out the murder scene?'

Charlie Grant looked at me hard. For a moment it looked like he was about to blurt something out, then apparently he had thought better of it and changed his mind. He simply turned his back on me and began walking up the stairs to the murder room. I followed a few steps behind him, slowly, carefully. Expecting something. Ready for anything. This was turning out to be one big stinking morning so far.

Upstairs there were four bedrooms. It was a large house and the rooms were large. One was the master bedroom. We found out that the wife was not home — thank God! I didn't feel like dealing with some hysterical grieving widow with her dead husband still in the next room just then. We were also informed there was a maid in the house, the uniforms had her waiting in the kitchen downstairs. We'd talk to her later.

Right now we checked out the upstairs rooms. The other three bedrooms weren't bedrooms at all. I was amazed to discover that each room was ringed on all sides from floor to ceiling with wooden shelving, which was loaded to the bursting point with all kinds of books. All over these rooms and even in the hallway were more shelves and more piles of books. There were stacks as tall as I was on the floor. We could hardly move.

'Damn books everywhere!' Grant muttered. 'This whole house is full of stinking books.'

'He's a book dealer,' I reminded Grant.

'Yeah, I got it, Hollow, but, I mean, this is crazy, man.'

I didn't say anything else. Grant was right for once — talk about obsessive and compulsive collecting — and I was a collector myself so I understood some of this. Still and all, it was just too much for me to deal with. The house was large but all the shelves and piles of books made it seem so much smaller, tighter, so constricted.

'Bet there's a small fortune here, though,' Grant added rhetorically, and I could see the greed wheels spinning in his crafty head. 'I mean, if a guy knew just which ones out of all these damn books were worth the big money . . . out of all this mess . . . '

The son-of-a-bitch was already making pilfering plans. That was another thing I didn't like about Charlie Grant. Guys that go into people's homes — some cops, firemen and home nurses — some seem to feel they can help themselves and pick up samples of whatever goodies they like — as long as the owner is a corpse, not home, or too old and incapacitated to even know they're being robbed blind.

I sighed, 'Come on, the vic is in this room here.'

Grant and I entered the largest room where there was an ornate wooden desk. This must have been Brian McDonald's office. Behind the desk, in an old wooden swivel chair, sat a dead man with a knife or letter opener in his back. Brian McDonald, an older looking guy, grey hair, balding, a little overweight but it didn't look bad on him — and very dead. I looked closer and saw that the weapon was indeed a letter opener, not a knife, and that it protruded from his back, just below the neck. Nicely placed. He died instantly.

Two guys from the crime lab squeezed by us and were taking photos, then started dusting for prints.

'We in your way?' I asked the older of the two, a guy named Ed Jenkins.

'Nah, we're almost done here. Place looks pretty clean' — then he laughed: 'I mean it's a mess, but I doubt we'll pick up any prints. First thing, we dusted the handle of the letter opener and it was clean of any prints, even the vic's, so it was wiped clean before it was used. The killer wasn't a pro but he knew what he was doing. He wore gloves.'

'I left the letter opener for you guys to see,' Jenkins said. 'We already took photos.'

Grant and I nodded and took a gander at the murder wound. It was grim, the letter opener dug deep into the flesh of the upper back.

'That must have hurt,' Grant offered with a wink to Ed Jenkins.

'I'll bet,' Jenkins laughed with his best graveside humour.

Now that we'd seen the murder weapon undisturbed, Jenkins carefully extracted it from McDonald's back with a gloved hand and deftly placed it in a clear plastic evidence bag.

'Anything else?' I asked Jenkins.

'Well, there's the message written on

the desktop. I mean, 'Book Collectors, Go To Hell!,' what the hell does that mean?'

'We don't know yet,' I said stumped. 'Ah, Ed, keep that quiet for now, okay?'

Jenkins gave me a twisted grin, 'Sure. Good luck with that! Anyway, the message was almost certainly written with one of these black sharpie markers here; we got prints off of them all, except one. I'd bet the other black markers have the prints of the victim, they were his markers after all. Wanna bet the one we found without any prints was used by the killer and was wiped clean? He knew what he was doing.'

I nodded. It all meant we had nothing yet.

'What about the books? Does it look like anything was stolen?' Grant asked.

Ed Jenkins just laughed at that, 'In all this mess? You kidding! Who could tell?'

I nodded, the wife might know, once we talked to her. I wondered where she was. What was keeping her from coming home? I told Grant I wanted to speak to the wife, when she came home from wherever she was, and anyone else closely associated with the victim.

'There's a Mexican maid downstairs,' Ed Jenkins reminded us as he and his partner packed up to leave. 'I told her to wait for you guys in the kitchen.'

'Thanks, Ed, we'll have a talk with her before we leave.'

Once the crime lab guys walked out, I saw them passing the guys from the morgue who were already waiting out in the hall to come in and take Brian McDonald's body away.

'Give us a few minutes, guys?'

'Yeah, take all the time you need, detectives,' one of the men replied with a wry smile. 'We're on the clock. No problemo.'

I looked at Charlie Grant — my partner — damnit! I slowly closed the office door so that we were now alone with the corpse. It was quiet in that room full of books, deathly quiet.

'So what do you think?'

So help me, Grant looked at me seriously and said, 'The guy's dead. Murdered.'

'That's a big help,' I said sarcastically.

'Look, Hollow, what the hell you want? We got nothing yet. Usual suspects, boyo, that's all. See who matches up, then we get our guy,' he said confidently.

'What do you make of the message written on the desk?'

'Book Collectors, Go To Hell?'

'Yeah, that message.'

'Who even knows it has anything to do with the murder?' he replied, and damn if he wasn't serious about it.

I didn't say anything for a moment, I was exasperated. I tried counting to ten before I replied. Finally I said, 'Look, I suppose it is within the realm of possibility that the message had nothing to do with the murder, but I don't buy it for a second.'

'So don't buy it, Hollow. What you want me to do about it. I didn't write it,' Grant replied getting all arrogant on me again.

''Book Collectors, Go To Hell!' doesn't fit in with the murder? Are you serious?' I asked incredulously.

'He wasn't a book collector.'

'What?' I asked astonished now.

'He wasn't a book collector, he was a book dealer. A bookseller. Well, wasn't he?'

'Well, yes, technically you're right, but in the collecting world that's sometimes a bit of a misnomer. In any field lots of collectors deal to support their collecting habit and a lot of dealers also collect themselves.'

'Whatever,' was Grant's brilliant reply.

I sighed, this guy was no help, barely even cooperative. 'So how do you want to go about this?'

'We talk to the maid downstairs, then the wife,' he said casually.

'Fine. Then we proceed from where they lead us?' I asked.

'That's it, Hollow, standard police work,' he couldn't resist jabbing me. 'Maybe in ten or twenty years you'll get the hang of it.'

Once we left the morgue guys came in to take away the body and Brian McDonald was gone forever.

2

Too Many Suspects

The maid was seated at the kitchen table waiting for us. She was an older Hispanic woman named Felipa Calderon, Mexican, and almost certainly illegal. She was nervous, scared stiff, wanting to be any place but where she was right now talking to two detectives about her murdered boss.

'What weel happen to me?' she asked in broken English. 'I need this job. I work for Mr. Brian for two years now. Good years.'

'You'll be okay,' I said softly. 'Now just tell us about the murder.'

'I know nothing,' she blurted, still fearful.

'Well, what did you see?' Grant barked. 'Come on, out with it or you'll be gone, on the bus back home. *Comprende*?'

'Easy on her,' I told Grant.

'You gotta get their attention, Hollow,

25

or she'll never spill. Put some fear in her and she'll tell what she saw.'

I turned to the maid and told her, 'Don't worry, Felipa, you won't get hurt in this, I promise you, just be truthful with us.' I looked over at Grant, 'Let me handle this.'

'I know nothing,' the maid repeated. Then at my urgings she added, 'I do my work, clean the house for Mrs. Milly, his wife. I never go into the book rooms, Mr. Brian forbid me to go in there. Too cluttered. I do not know how he can work in there. So much books, piles of books, everywhere. I offered to clean it for him one day and he told me no. No. No!'

'So how did you find the body?' Grant asked suspiciously. 'If you said you never went into those rooms?'

Felipa looked at Grant fearfully, 'I seen him slumped over at his desk when I pass by in the hallway. I bring up towels for the bathroom. I thought Mr. Brian was sleeping, I called out to him, then *Madre de Dios*, I saw the knife sticking in his back.'

'Letter opener,' I corrected.

'*Si*, it was his letter opener. The silver

one from his desk.'

'And then?' I prompted.

'Then I call *la policia*,' she said simply. 'Will I lose my job now?'

Grant shook his head impatiently and ignored her.

I looked at Felipa, 'I don't know, you'll have to talk that over with Mrs. McDonald. By the way where is Mrs. McDonald? We need to talk to her.'

'I do not know,' the maid snapped a bit too quickly and I could see she was lying, covering up. But what and why?

'She knows something,' Grant told me glomming onto the scent like a blood-hound. To me he was just stating the obvious but I didn't comment.

'Where's Mrs. McDonald?' I asked Felipa.

'I no know nothing,' she told me quickly. It was clear she was scared of saying where the wife was. Something was going on.

'We'll come back to her later,' I told Grant and he nodded.

'Yeah, once we find her. We need to talk to the wife,' Grant added.

I looked at Felipa and asked her, 'So

who do you think killed Mr. McDonald?'

The maid hardly hesitated in her response, 'Oh, it was certainly Mrs. McDonald. She hated him, he was cheating on her with a Black woman. Always the Black women with Mr. Brian.'

'Ah!' Charlie Grant burst out impatiently smelling another scent now, one more to his liking containing scandal and sex. This time I decided to let him run with it for just a little bit to see where it might lead us. 'So Felipa, Mr. Brian liked the Black women?'

'*Si*, before me he had a *negrita* maid, Alice Larkin, but Miss Milly caught them. So Alice was fired. She was very angry with Mr. Brian.'

'Miss Milly or Miss Larkin?' I asked.

'Oh, both! Both very angry at him,' she said shaking her head in disapproval.

'Well, that's two suspects,' Grant said.

I shrugged, apparently so, but we'd have to check this all out a lot more deeply before we could rule anyone in, or out.

'But Mr. Brian always fighting, have many enemies, always troubles in book business,' she added. 'It's a crazy, *loco* business.'

'What other enemies?' I asked fishing for information. Felipa was openly talking to us now and she had apparently turned into a veritable gold mine of valuable information I hoped — or a dead-end rumor mill — or maybe both. I wanted to keep her talking, then I'd lead her back to the subject of the whereabouts of Mrs. McDonald.

'Mr. Brian have a partner, name of Spears, and they always argue, each one accuse the other of stealing. I don't know how they can be in business together. Mr. Brian's ex-wife, Sandy — such a nice lady, but sad. I met her once. I hear he treated her terrible. Then Mr. Johns of Royal Books, Mr. Brian tell me once they have a big feud that runs for 20 years! Imagine that?'

I looked at Grant, 'We got enough here for three murder cases.'

'Seems like that,' he admitted grimly. Then Grant ran them off on his fingers one by one. 'We got the wife, the ex-wife, the former Black maid he got caught *schtooking*, the crooked business partner, then the feud with his main competitor in the book business. Anyone else?'

The question had been rhetorical but Felipa shrugged, 'Mr. Brian was a very complicated man.'

'So it seems,' I said. 'Now he's dead.'

'Yes,' she replied as if she still did not believe it.

'Now, Felipa, where is Mrs. McDonald?' I asked sternly.

She looked up at me, 'Oh, please, do not make me tell you that. It will cause much trouble. When she come home, she will tell you everything.'

'Look you!' Grant barked, 'tell us now or I swear I'll take you out of here!'

Felipa looked at me with pleading eyes. I looked at Charlie Grant, I knew he was bluffing, the last thing he wanted to do was bring in anyone unless it was the actual killer. He saw anything else as just one big annoyance. 'Forget about her for now. The wife will turn up soon, then we'll get what we need from her.'

'I don't know, Hollow,' Grant said. 'I don't like it.'

'Come on, let's go.'

3

The Ex-Wife

We left the maid. She was very happy to see us go. By that time the morgue guys had already taken the body out of the house. Meanwhile, the wife still hadn't come home and it appeared she could not be found. I began to wonder why. I also began to wonder just what the maid knew and what she was covering up.

Just to be on the safe side Grant and I put out an APB on the wife, her physical description, make and model of her car. Her car was missing too. I was beginning to get a bad feeling about this case. Was the wife the killer? Or was she already dead, her body rotting away in the trunk of her car somewhere in long-term parking over at the airport?

Felipa had told us that she thought the wife was the killer — but really, was it true? Felipa had also fingered a bunch of other people as the possible killer — so what could we believe of Felipa's words? Probably nothing.

Grant and I went through McDonald's address book for info on all the people Felipa had mentioned. We decided to go and see the ex-wife first.

On the drive over, Grant and I chewed over the case.

'So what do you think?' I asked him.

'Why do you always ask me what I think, Hollow? I don't think anything,' the empty-headed moron told me gruffly, he was driving and getting impatient. It was obvious he didn't even want to talk to me and that our argument of the morning still rankled. I couldn't blame him for that but we still had to be professional, we still had to work together if we were to solve this case. It was becoming increasingly difficult for me to work with Grant, and vice versa.

I decided to prod him a bit, 'So you have nothing on your mind?'

'No, nothing, *nada*, zilch, you got it?' he replied sharply.

'That's just great!' I said trying to hold

my temper in check.

According to Felipa, Sandy Goddard was the ex-wife of Brian McDonald. She had been his first wife. They had been married for 15 years, then divorced three years ago and from Felipa we got the feeling the divorce had not gone very well. But as we found out, not all was as Felipa told us. Either she was outright lying; the language problem got in the way, or she only saw a small part of the total picture. Probably she did not truly know the full truth at all.

Felipa did let on to us one little bit of info that Grant found interesting. When I'd asked Felipa if she knew of any hanky-panky between Mr. Brian and his ex-wife — the type of thing a current wife might not appreciate very much — she told us, 'Oh, no, Miss Sandy not like the mens any longer. She likes womens only now. I do not understand this, but she is a nice lady, she always good to me.'

'Lezbo!' was all Charlie Grant had said then.

I looked at him askance but kept mum. It was a long quiet ride.

We eventually pulled up to the apartment house where Sandy Goddard lived. It was a moderate pile of brick and mortar in a less than affluent section of town. The gal seemed to be on hard times since she'd split with her husband, how hard we'd soon find out. I'd called ahead so Ms. Goddard was already waiting for us when we rang her bell.

She greeted us with a large smile, and she had the body to go along with it. She was a large woman; tall and rather stately with a nice figure, a bit of an Amazon princess type with a top thatch of bright short red hair. I liked what I saw, and I could see Charlie Grant was digging her too.

I decided it was best to put away any interest I felt and get down to business right away. I told her that her ex-husband was dead.

Goddard looked shocked, disbelief and then sadness covering her face. Suddenly she blurted, 'Brian, dead? Oh, no . . . oh my God, no!'

She burst into tears. I looked at her carefully, it didn't seem like an act. Had

Felipa been wrong? I wondered about that now. It was obvious the ex-wife still had strong feelings for Brian McDonald. I also wondered if any woman would ever cry like that for me when she heard that I had died. Probably not.

Charlie Grant went and sat down next to the woman, trying to console her, putting his arms around her and then rubbing her shoulders, her neck, her waist. I began to wonder just what the hell he was doing, because it was beginning to look like he was giving her a full body message. She certainly had a full, robust body, tailor-made for it. I shook my head, realizing what had begun as a seemingly innocent gesture by Grant had become totally inappropriate.

Sandy Goddard suddenly noted what Grant was doing and began to look very uncomfortable. She looked over at me.

I knew I had to step in somehow. 'Grant, I think this would be a good time for you to get Ms. Goddard a glass of water. I'm sure she'd appreciate that.'

My partner looked at me sharply, but then got up and went into the kitchenette.

'Ms. Goddard,' I continued, quickly changing the subject from sexual harassment of a witness — or a suspect — back to normal police business, 'I know this has been a big shock to you, and we are sorry for your loss. If you can, try to compose yourself, because we really need to ask you some questions.'

'Yes', she stammered, making an effort to regain control.

'Your ex-husband was murdered and we need to find the killer.'

She looked shocked, once more tried to dry her tears with a shirt sleeve, looked at me in evident surprise, 'Murdered?'

'Yes, he was stabbed to death, sometime last evening.'

'My God, poor Brian.' she said between sniffles she was valiantly trying to hold back. 'That's so terrible.'

'Yes it is,' I replied. There didn't seem to be anything else to say.

Grant came back into the living room with a glass of water and she took it gratefully, sipping slowly, 'Thank you, Detective.'

Grant leered down at her, lusting eyes taking inventory of her body, the low-cut blouse that showed her ample breasts, though I was sure that in her grief, Ms. Goddard hardly noticed. At least I hoped so. Then Grant ruined it all when he said, 'Think nothing of it, sweet thing.'

Ms. Goddard looked up at Charlie Grant suspiciously then. I cleared my throat quickly to get her attention. 'Ah, Ms. Goddard, can you tell us where you were yesterday evening?'

That took her attention away from my partner, thank God. Grant didn't even suspect I had saved his ass from big trouble, he just leered at me, his eyes telling me to lay off and stop interfering with his play.

I looked over at Ms. Goddard, waiting. 'Well, I was . . . ' she looked at me closely for the first time and then asked, 'Am I a suspect, Detective?'

'Everyone is a suspect, ma'am,' I said with a wan smile. 'We have to ask everyone the question. So do you have an alibi for where you were last night?

'Of course, I was away, out of the city at a resort upstate. I can verify it all,' she told me.

'And what's the name of the guy you were with?' Grant asked. I looked at him sharply and he just grinned, like the fool he was. I waited for the other foot to drop. I didn't have long to wait.

Sandy Goddard smiled coyly, 'The resort is a lesbian retreat, Detective, but I am sure I can give you the names of plenty of women who saw me there all day and all evening.'

I sighed, 'All right, we'll get back to that.' I quickly changed tack. 'Can you think of anyone who would want to kill your ex-husband?'

Goddard suddenly laughed, 'That's a good one! Who wouldn't want to kill Brian, might be a better question.'

'Does that include you?' I asked her.

'No, Brian and I decided to go our separate ways a long time ago, even while we were married. I did not care what he did after I found out about his cheating on me that first time. Our divorce was amicable enough and he treated me rather well in the settlement,' she said softly. 'I'm afraid I spent my settlement too lavishly, wasted it, in fact on trips and travel, but that's hardly Brian's fault. We even stayed friends.'

'Really?' Grant asked suspiciously.

'Yes, really, Detective,' Goddard told him boldly. 'You may not understand, but some people can be adult about even the most personal things. Brian and I understood each other, we got along better after the divorce than when we had been married.'

Grant just shook his head. I looked at her, trying to figure her out and coming up empty. She seemed like she was telling the truth. She also seemed to be a decent enough person, whatever that means today. Maybe she was even telling us the truth. Stranger things can happen.

'All right, then can you think of anyone else who would want to kill your ex-husband?' I repeated.

'Well, there's so many,' she said, shaking her head sadly.

'Can you explain that?' Grant asked, looking at me sharply. I could see his frustration with the woman was growing, as his libido regarding her was probably shrinking.

Sandy Goddard smiled sweetly, ignored Grant and spoke directly to me, 'Detective, I'd look at that bitch of a wife of his for starters. Milly. She is an evil, money-grubbing whore. Pardon my French. Brian's partner, that man Spears, I never liked him, I think he is a crook and a pervert. Then there's one of Brian's major competitors, another bookseller, a big fat guy who thinks he's some tough Mafia wannabe by the way he acts. I think he could be dangerous. I never liked him.'

I nodded, taking notes, asking for the names and the spellings of them along with addresses and phone numbers. She gave us what she had.

'And what about you?' Grant asked again. 'You mean to tell me that there was no animosity when you and your husband split up?'

'No, it's just as I told you, we had been going our separate ways for a few years. Brian was deep into his book thing. I never understood it, but he made a lot of money doing it; he had a lot of customers. They were always looking to buy and make deals. I didn't understand

40

it all, or care about it, really. I don't collect books. I don't collect anything. I hate clutter. So we just split and went our separate ways. Brian was generous in the divorce, he didn't argue or make trouble for me. He gave me half the assets and the old house.'

'I see,' I said thinking it through. She seemed truthful. 'I see you're living in lower circumstances here than he was?'

'Yes, as I said, I had a financial reversal, it was silly really. I put most of my divorce money into a local business and then promptly lost it all when they went under. Brian did well in his book business though, and told me he sold a lot of big money items. We remained friends and spoke on the phone now and then. So he was able to afford the new bigger house, the new trophy bitch-wife and even an occasional mistress on the side. That was so like Brian. Oh, yes, Detectives, he let on to me about them too, male bragging, no doubt. Brian works very hard and is doing very well for himself but he enjoys his pleasures.'

'*Did* enjoy,' Grant reminded her.

She did not reply, but she glared at Grant. Good, I thought, I felt like bitch-slapping his ugly mug but steeled myself to concentrate on the work at hand.

'What about his books?' I asked.

'Well,' she said softly — did I see just a hint of discomfort come to her features — 'I never took any interest in them. So I let him have them all in the settlement. I realize now that it was probably a mistake for me financially but I didn't care about them that much — not then — and Brian did so love his books. So as far as I was concerned he could have them all. I was just glad to be free of *him* — and *them* — and I got the house and some cash so I was happy.'

Sandy Goddard sat quietly looking out the window, thinking; maybe about Brian, maybe about the passing years. She looked sad. I wondered about her. She was either the best damn actress I'd ever run across in 25 years of police work — and I'd run across a few, let me tell you! — or she still had genuine feelings for the dead man and her waters ran a lot deeper than I'd first thought. Brian and her, after all, had been married for 15 years. That's a long, long time. Beth and I hadn't lasted nowhere near that long before she'd run off with her rich doctor, but I could see how these things went. I still missed Beth sometimes. Brian's ex-wife, Sandy, didn't seem like a bad egg, in spite of her lesbian proclivities. She was an ex-wife who still missed her ex-husband; you can't make this stuff up. It was sad, really.

There wasn't much more to ask Ms. Goddard now and it was getting late. Tomorrow is another day, as Scarlett O'Hara was so fond of saying in *Gone With The Wind*, and Grant and I had a full plate of interviews lined up for the next day's work. First among them was with Milly, Brian's present wife, who it appeared had finally turned up and was ready to talk.

Grant and I said our goodbyes to Ms. Goddard and called it a day.

4

The Value Book

The next morning I met Charlie Grant in the squad room and we filled in Captain Wallace on what we had, and what we had done up to then. It wasn't much but we told him we were hoping for better success today. Then we took a ride out to the McDonald house to talk to the wife, Mildred, aka Milly.

Brian McDonald's body had been taken away the previous day and we discovered that Milly McDonald had returned home later that evening. She'd heard the news of her husband's murder on the TV news. She was in the house with her mother and sister, both of whom were there to console her. Her being the grieving widow and all and seemingly playing it for all it was worth.

We got her away from the family and put our questions to her. She was in

44

shock, or at least that's what she told us, but she sure didn't appear all that upset. She said she had no problem talking to us.

'I'm sorry about your husband,' I began, looking her over carefully. She was a petite blonde, with a slim, nice figure, a smaller-sized version of his first wife. Brian seemed to do pretty good for himself with the ladies — his women so far were not the usual type of hefty-sized gals teamed up with most bookmen. But then, McDonald had made a lot of money his ex-wife had told us by selling high-end expensive books and various associational items to wealthy clients — so Milly was the new trophy wife. She sure looked it.

'Yes, I will miss Brian,' was her only reply. She sat there looking appropriately sad I thought, but with no tears, not like the ex-wife had shown us. This woman was a cold one, for sure.

Charlie Grant looked at me hard and I could see his lips slowly spell out the word B.I.T.C.H.

I shrugged, well maybe the ex-wife had

been right about the new wife, but the ex was hardly the person to give an unbiased judgment on the matter. Nevertheless, Milly McDonald seemed to me to be as cold as ice. To be sure, she looked very nice on the outside, but she seemed impatiently nasty, someone who seemed to feel royally entitled, and for the first time I began to feel sorry for Mr. Brian, as Felipa the maid called him. Brian McDonald may have made a big mistake leaving his first wife for this new, younger model.

'Yes,' I responded to her words, 'I'm sure that a lot of people will miss your husband. Now, can you tell us where you were yesterday and the night of the murder? We were looking for you all day. Can you tell us where you were and what you were doing?'

She shifted in the seat uncomfortably, 'My alibi? Is that it? You consider me to be a suspect in my own husband's death?'

'Murder,' I reminded her.

'Everyone is a suspect at this point,' Grant said wearily.

'Very well, you'll find out sooner or

later. I imagine that Mexican maid, Lupe or whatever her name is, probably told you all about it already.'

'No,' I said quickly. 'Felipa told us nothing.'

'Oh, well, then good, I'm glad she knows her place. Anyway, you want to know where I was, I was away with Rodolfo,' she said casually. A bit too casually for my taste.

'Rodolfo?' I asked.

She cleared her throat, 'My pool boy. We were . . . what would you call it, Detective . . . ? There must be some suitably tawdry word to describe it. I'm sure you know all about such things. We were at the Holiday Inn on Route 12, all day and all night.'

'Shacked-up, eh?' Grant said with a lascivious leer. This was his kind of alibi and I was sure he wanted to know all the details. 'I guess you can prove that?'

'Yes, if I must. I have hotel credit card receipts, the desk clerk who signed us in knows us as regulars, it will be no problem.'

'And where were you the night your

husband was murdered?' I asked. 'You were not in the house and the maid was asleep,'

She smiled, 'With Rodolfo, of course. We have a regular thing, he is insatiable.'

I nodded, but I figured she had the facts about who was insatiable reversed.

She smiled, 'So now you know it all.'

I sighed, 'Okay, Mrs. McDonald, I'm not concerned about your and Brian's relationships, so long as they don't figure into this investigation, but I don't want anything to impede the solving of his murder.'

She nodded. 'Well, Brian was cheating on me too, you know. Cheating with some Black woman. I'd even caught him once, doing one of the maids in my own house. In our own bed! He was totally out of control. I think he was some kind of sex addict. You know how they can be. After that, there was no love lost between us. I was just staying here waiting for my divorce to become final so I could get half his damn books.'

'Books?' Grant asked curiously. 'You mean you wanted half of the house and the cash? Not books?'

'No, Detective. I said books and I meant books. The house is under a double mortgage and has almost no equity. Brian had little money in the bank, and less cash in hand. His true wealth was in the book collection, which is what is worth the big money. All his money went into it. It is worth a million dollars, I believe. Maybe millions of dollars!'

Charlie Grant whistled loudly, 'Damn!'

'Millions?' I asked, incredulous. It hardly seemed possible. I looked at her closely. The greed oozed off her like sweat on a hot summer day. I figured her values for the books were way over-inflated, much like the spouses of too many collectors who always think the collection they have inherited is priceless. It may well be priceless, but not in the way they think it is — which only means cold cash to them. I figured McDonald's books may not be worth anywhere near what his wife thought they were worth.

'Probably a million dollars, who can tell. I'd have to look them up, each and every one of them,' she explained. Then with a smile she added, 'I was to get half of them in the settlement, now that he's dead, it looks like I get them all.'

I looked at Grant and he allowed a brief shiver — she was one cold cookie.

'But there's something I don't understand. With so many thousands of books here — I mean this house is loaded to the rafters with them — how can you tell which books are worth money and how much each one is worth?' I asked.

'Oh. Brian had his Value Book. It is a thick binder he kept up to date religiously. In it he wrote data on every single book he had that was worth big money. There are thousands of them. Do you know how many of them are valued in the five figures? Anyway, he also listed in there what he paid for each book, where he got it, and what each one is worth in the present market. He kept up with sales and auction results from all the major houses. Everything is in that book.'

'So where is this Value Book?' I asked.

Mrs. McDonald shrugged, 'Gone? Missing? Lost? Who knows? When I heard what happened last night I ran upstairs to

Brian's office . . . '

'Where he was murdered?' Grant added sharply.

'Yes,' she replied hardly missing a beat, not even looking at him, or me. 'I went up to get it. It was gone. Brian always kept it laying in the centre of the top of his desk.'

'Right where someone wrote that message.' I said softly.

She nodded, 'Brian was a very neat man. Orderly. Everything had a place and was always kept in its place. Now I discovered that everything usually on his desk was thrown to the floor and someone had written that crazy statement about book collectors. Brian wasn't even a book collector,' she said sharply.

Grant looked at me with a 'I told you so' look.

''Book Collectors, Go To Hell!'' I reminded her.

'Yes, can you believe it?' She laughed, then added: 'Well, if you knew Brian, and some of those book collector people he dealt with, that statement may actually be accurate. They're an odd bunch. Brian certainly was.'

'So what does that message mean to you?' I asked her.

She looked at me blankly, 'I really have no idea.'

'So this Value Book is still missing?' I continued.

'Yes, it's strange, it's nowhere to be found in his office. Brian never let it out of his sight, it never left that room. I think it may have been stolen.'

'By the murderer?' Grant asked, I could see he was egging her on.

Milly McDonald shrugged, 'I guess so. I certainly don't have it and it's not anywhere in this house — and believe me — I've looked! That's my meal ticket.'

How nice, I thought. I was going to ask her if she'd killed her husband, but then remembered she'd told us about her alibi — which we'd check out soon enough. But something just told me that her alibi was good, it wasn't even worth looking at her for this. If she'd done it, Brian would have disappeared, never to be seen or heard from again. No, this had to be the handiwork of someone else. Maybe his partner or an upset client?

Grant and I were both back at square one but we did know one thing — that Value Book was important, it was missing, and the killer probably took it!

'We find that Value Book,' I told Grant on the way out to our car, 'and we find our killer.'

'I'd like to get my hands on that book too,' Grant said grimly but somehow I didn't think his reasons were the same as my own.

* * *

Next on our list of persons of interest, as they say, was Brian's partner in McDonald & Spears Rare Books, Alex Spears. However, before we left the McDonald house, we had a chance to speak with Rodolfo, the pool boy. He was a good-looking young man, tailor-made for the gigolo role. He corroborated the wife's story in every detail. He even showed us photos! They were very provocative.

'Mrs. McDonald knows about these?' I asked Rodolfo.

'Of course, it was her idea,' the pool

53

boy responded with a wide grin.

Grant looked them over carefully, then put some in his pocket claiming he needed them for evidence. I didn't want to think about it.

'So the wife and the pool boy?' Grant said later as I drove us over to Alex Spears' address. That was McDonald's partner. Grant ran though his notes and added, 'So we got this Brian McDonald and the former maid — Ayesha Hedger — and the new mistress — Alice Larkin. Then we've got the bitchy current wife and the lesbo ex-wife. Quite the messy life our Brian led. What is it with these book collectors, Hollow?'

I shrugged, like I could answer his question. I could see Grant was stymied. This case was beginning to give me a headache too. I was wondering how it would eventually settle out. Would we ever find out who the killer was? And why murder Brian McDonald? Was it really for his damn books? That was just too weird to believe, even for book collectors, I thought.

And where was that Value Book now?

That surely had to be the key to it all.

We met Brian McDonald's partner, Alex Spears, at his home on the other side of town. It was another large house but not so luxurious as the one we'd just left. There was no pool, no pool boy, and no maid; only a big empty house — except for the books — the place was full to the brim with books. Books all over the damn place! Shelved, stacked in piles on the floor, some of the piles as tall as I was.

And cats. Cats everywhere and into everything!

We'd called ahead and Spears let us in and escorted us inside carefully to his office, another room like all the other rooms in the house with shelves that ran from floor to ceiling stuffed tightly with books. I walked among the stacks gingerly, fearful of causing some type of book tsunami. There were all kinds of books, everywhere, all over. Most of them were wrapped in some kind of clear plastic covering, or in clear plastic bags. It was worse than McDonald's place. We were surrounded and could hardly move.

Then there were the cats. If I thought

the book clutter was bad, the cats made it worse. They were everywhere too, sitting on the tops of piles of books and looking at us like we were enemy interlopers, or chasing each other between the stacks, meowing and clawing at each other. Sometimes they knocked down stacks of books to the floor with a resounding crash.

'I hate when they do that,' Spears told us as he got up to rearrange the stacks or put a fallen book back in its proper place on a shelf or atop some pile.

The smell of cat piss was the worst part of it all. I mean the odour was overwhelming, pungent and sharp. It was bad. The cats seemed to have free run of the place. I wondered if there was some unwritten law about books and cats existing in some symbiotic relationship. I knew Grant hated cats, so that made it more bearable for me to be there. I was actually enjoying his discomfit.

'Terrible news about Brian,' Alex Spears told us once we were seated as comfortably as possible, in his tightly cramped office. He was smoking a pipe and the rich cherry flavour thankfully covered up some of the strong feline odour in the room that threatened to overcome us at any moment. I could see that Grant was none too happy and wanted to get out of there as soon as possible. I couldn't blame him, but we needed to have a good long talk with Spears first.

I looked around me, taking in the full impact of the room. It was actually rather large, but seemed so small with all the shelves. I only learned later that all of them were double shelves, where the books were placed on them in two or even three rows. The piles of books all around us made me feel like a western pioneer in a covered wagon surrounded by attacking Indians. We were surrounded and we could hardly move at all. The effect was very claustrophobic. The cat smell was getting to me too now. I wanted out as soon as I could and Grant just held his nose and cursed under his breath.

'We need to ask you a few questions, Mr. Spears,' I began.

He nodded affably, 'Ask away. Sorry

about all my little friends here. I just can't resist cats and kittens, and they all go along so well with my books.'

'How many of these cats you got here?' Grant asked in amazement.

'Oh, my cats? Probably twenty, but some keep dying on me and then others get born, so it fluctuates.'

I grinned with joy when I saw Grant frantically pick up a big fat tabby cat that had suddenly clawed his way up his leg to flop upon his lap like he owned my partner, and Grant quickly threw it to the ground in angry disdain.

'That's my Mr. Poe,' Spears said with a smile full of pride.

'Mr. Poe?' Grant growled, quickly brushing cat hair off his suit.

'Yes, Mr. Edgar Allan Poe. All my cats are named after famous authors,' Spears said proudly. 'Mr. Poe is really very friendly, loves to be petted, not at all like that damn Hemingway, he is just trouble, trouble, trouble! Watch out for him, I warn you.'

I looked around suspiciously, imagining Hemingway laying somewhere unseen ready to spring at me in ambush.

'Yes,' Spears continued, 'they really are an active bunch. Mary Shelley had a litter of three, H. P. Lovecraft, Dashiell Hammett and Raymond Chandler. John Steinbeck or Ian Fleming impregnated both Agatha Christie and Louisa May Alcott, begetting C. S. Forester, Victor Hugo, Mickey Spillane and Robert E. Howard. Howard recently died, he was much too young, just like in real life.'

I looked at Spears incredulous as he continued.

'Charles Dickens is really a very nice fellow, for a cat, a true gentleman and A. C. Doyle and his brother — he's the only cat I allow not named after an author — Sherlock Holmes — are a friendly pair. Emily Dickinson begot John Dickson Carr, Max Brand, and Geoffrey Chaucer. The oldest cat I have is Old Homer, I've had him for nearly 12 years. I think that sums them up,' Spears finished.

'How nice,' Grant replied sarcastically. 'You know, you're a very sick man. Do you know that?'

I saw that Spears looked hurt and I

couldn't but help feel sorry for the old guy. It was obvious all he had in the world were his books and his cats. I wondered if the cats peed all over the books but though I looked, I didn't see evidence of that. They were probably all fixed but the cat boxes on the floors of every room made the smell pretty bad. I decided to change the subject to focus more on the reason we were there in the first place, hoping to get away from cats and the cat smell.

'What about the books, Mr. Spears?' I continued looking around me in awe. He was an older man, small sized, and as I looked at him I could foresee the day, when he, or one of his cats, would run into a stack of books that would knock over all the other stacks. Then he might end up being buried alive under hundreds of pounds of books. Death by books! I shook my head, that was weird; the claustrophobic atmosphere and breathing all that strong cat box stink must have got to me a lot more than I realized. I was amazed that it didn't seem to bother him at all.

'Oh, the books, now that's different. I have exactly 35, 145 hard covers, 505 bedsheet magazines, 3,500 slick magazines, 250 vintage newspapers, 2,000 various digestsize magazines, 1,850 pulp magazines, 45 boxes of various manuscripts and ephemera, and some 95,000 paperback books of all sizes and formats — give or take a dozen.' he said proudly.

'You counted them all?' Grant asked incredulous, shaking his head in disbelief.

'I keep very precise sales records, sir.' Spears shot back sharply but I couldn't tell by his tone if he was proud or insulted by what Grant had asked him. 'Accurate records are the heart and soul of success in the book business.'

I nodded, it made sense. I was a Depression glassware collector myself so I understood the collecting mentality. It could get a bit kooky sometimes, but these book people, they seemed to extend the term 'odd' into undiscovered realms of weirdness.

I saw Grant idly pick up a book that was laying on Spears desk, he hefted it in his hand as though trying to guess its weight like some carnival barker. It certainly looked like some old, poor condition relic, almost falling apart in Grant's hands. If Spears was selling junk like this, he sure couldn't be making any money in the book business.

'Be careful with that! Put it down now!' Spears shouted at Grant, suddenly very angry. 'My God, be careful, that's so delicate you can damage it easily. Then I'll have to mark it down from 'Good' to only 'Fair'.'

Grant dropped the book back on the desk, 'This old thing?'

Spears fumed, made an effort to calm himself, then picked up the book and held it carefully in his hands, away from us and out of our reach. Then he said with exaggerated feeling, 'This old *thing*, is a thing of beauty, a rare and lovely volume, it is *A Pearl of Great Price* by Joseph Smith.'

'Yeah? So what?' Grant said with a shrug.

'So what!' Spears actually growled at us. 'So what! You, young man, are a dolt!'

'Easy, Mr. Spears, maybe you can explain to us the significance of this book?' I asked, hoping Grant was too inundated by claustrophobia and cat smell to do anything to the old man at being called a name. I allowed a thin smile, maybe Grant didn't even know the word 'dolt' was an insult? I watched Grant cover his nose and mouth with his handkerchief as he mumbled menacingly.

Spears nodded, all of a sudden serious, 'Yes, all right. This book is very rare, it is the third book written by Joseph Smith, the founder of the Church of Jesus Christ of Latter Day Saints.'

'The Mormons?' I asked, trying to show him that I knew something about something.

'Correct,' Spears said quickly, now taking the role of schoolteacher to us dunderheaded students. 'This particular book is a rare British edition from 1851, originally it was published in wraps, that essentially means it is an early paperback. Even allowing its present worn condition, it is conservatively estimated to be worth from $30,000 to $50,000.'

Grant looked at the old man, then at the old book in his hands with eyes bulging. 'You're kidding me?'

'No, Smith's first book was *The Book of Mormon* which founded the religion, and is even more rare of course.'

'Of course,' I said.

Spears looked at me sharply, 'But this edition is quite unique, being the first British reprint of his third book about Mormonism.'

I gulped thoughtfully and looked over at Grant.

'All that dough for just one book?' Grant stammered in wonder, looking back at me in disbelief.

'For one book?' I repeated, suddenly realizing that there might be a lot more to this rare book business than I had ever expected. The collector in me was really paying attention now. This was nothing like the glassware field, at least not the field I knew about. This was big money, the type of money people killed for! And big profits, at least it looked that way to me. I might have to take a serious look at what opportunities there were in this collecting area. Maybe I'd speak to Spears about it in more depth after this case was over.

Alex Spears took the book and carefully placed it in a clear plastic bag and then put it high up on a shelf, away from us, no doubt. 'I just got it today from a dealer in England who had no idea what he had. Lucky me, but not every day is Christmas in this business, let me tell you. There's a lot of lean times between the rare flush times. I was just taking the book out of the Fed Ex box when you rang my doorbell. I didn't even have time to bag it yet.'

'Yeah, what a damn shame you didn't get a chance to bag it,' Grant added sarcastically.

I ignored Grant. 'Mr. Spears can you tell us about Brian McDonald and your business together?'

'Sure,' Spears replied lightly, now that his precious book was safe from us barbarians. When you got right down to it, he seemed like an odd but agreeable sort, friendly in his own way, willing to talk. I just hoped that he would have some good stuff to tell us. He began it by telling us, 'Brian and I were in the rare book business for 30 years, so long ago.

We were partners since college days. In fact, Brian put himself through college by buying and selling books. He was that good. After a few years we began to make some nice money dealing in high-end first editions, manuscripts and letters, even hyper moderns. As you can see we each keep our own stock in our own homes, selling by appointment only. It's worked out better for us that way. Brian's death is a tragic loss to the field, but it was not entirely unexpected.'

My ears perked up at that. 'How so?'

'Yeah?' Grant blurted, scenting something other than cat piss for the first time since we'd entered the house. 'Now let's get to the nitty-gritty.'

'Well, I mean, it was the life he led. I mean, for a bookman, Brian was all over the place; wife, ex-wife, mistress, even doing the maid and then getting caught doing it. What a mess! He told me all about it of course,' Spears said with a rather lascivious leer. 'He liked the Black women but always married White. Strange really, most bookmen I know prefer Asian women. Oh well, regardless,

66

it must be confusing being so sexually promiscuous and having to keep so many stories straight with so many different women. He was always like that, even in his college days, and it got him into no end of trouble. I remember one irate husband that swore to kill him . . .'

'Husbands too?' Grant mumbled in exaggerated awe.

'Oh, yes, but that was many years ago, Detective.'

'Mr. Spears let's concentrate on the here and now. Who do you think would want Brian McDonald dead?' I asked simply.

'Oh, well . . . almost everyone. We all hated him. Even me. He could be such a *putz*. He was cheating me in the business, you know. We were supposed to split the profits on every book we sold equally, after expenses. He never did. Oh, he'd send me a cheque now and then for a few hundred dollars, but that was just to keep me quiet. But I knew he was selling in the tens of thousands of dollars, steadily on a weekly basis, sir.'

'Really?' Grant blurted curiously. 'The

guy was pulling in that much moola?'

I looked at Spears, 'Is there really that much money to be made in bookselling?'

Spears laughed, 'Certainly not only in rare books, any kind of books, sir, if you have the right ones. Most bookmen I know are collectors, they only sell books because they love books. It's that simple. They love the book business, that means they love matching the right book with the right reader or collector. They use the money they make to buy more books! Brian was different, he was all about money — and of course sex and women. But he did have a gift. It was like he instinctively knew the best price he could get for any book and then match it to the perfect buyer. Sometimes the only buyer! It was like magic. The key was, he knew collectors and had the contacts, and of course, he had the books people wanted. I don't know how he got them, or where he got them, but he had them, that's for sure. Brian was a crook and a con man, a weasel and a cheat, but one hell of a bookman.'

'So who do you think killed him?' Grant asked impatiently, all this book talk was bugging him.

'You mean aside form me?' Spears asked with a wink and a nod. The guy was playing with us now and I could see that it was getting Grant pissed off — which I rather liked.

'Yeah,' I said, 'aside from you.'

'Well, I mean, isn't it obvious . . . ?' he told us with obvious simplicity.

By then Grant had had enough of him and his books. I saw he was still covering his nose from the cat stink, then he shouted, 'No, it is not obvious! Now are you going to talk sense or do I take you downtown!'

'Downtown? Booked for murder?' Spears almost smiled, and damn if he didn't look positively excited by the prospect. 'Why, that would certainly be interesting. I've never been 'downtown' before. Never! News of it would be sure to help my business — some good notorious publicity — I'm sure it would improve my sales of crime fiction and true crime. I specialize in those fields, Detective.'

I sighed, this was getting us nowhere. I began to wonder if the guy was crazy, or just crazy like a fox. 'So look, all kidding aside. Do you have any idea who would want Brian dead?'

Alex Spears nodded, 'Aside from almost everyone who knew him, or anyone he ever ran across, detective, sure, I can tell you who did it if you want.'

'Yes!' Grant shouted full of anger. 'That's what we want! Spill it!'

Spears looked at my partner carefully, a bit leery at his impatient outburst. 'It has to be his wife, Milly. Yes, certainly. Brian even mentioned it to me a couple of weeks ago. He said she wanted to divorce him and take all his books.'

'Is that right?' I asked.

'Yes, imagine that! She wanted to take *all* his books. I mean, if I had a wife and she was going to take *all* my books, I'd have to kill her too. I surely would. She would leave me no choice.' Spears spoke seriously, and damn if it didn't look like he meant every word of what he'd just told us. Then he added with a smile, 'I mean, if someone is going to take *all* of a man's books — what else is there for a man to do?'

'You're right about that,' a sarcastic Grant blurted angry now, annoyed and ready to get the hell out of there.

I shook my head, 'Thank you, Mr. Spears,' then I got up to leave. I'd had enough myself, and the cat smell had finally gotten to me, to the point where I was actually dizzy.

'But,' Spears added quickly, mysteriously, 'it could have been his chief competitor, Andy Johns. Johns stole one of his high-end clients and was moving in on Brian's territory. It could very well have been Johns. Those two were always at each others throats.'

I just nodded, Grant looked at Spears like he wanted to strangle him. At that point, I wasn't even sure I'd interfere if Grant decided to act upon that impulse.

'Then of course, there is Fred Smith, a real whale in the book world, high-end collector, spends a lot of money. He complained that Brian ripped him off on a big six-figure edition just last month. He said the book was woefully misrepresented. He swore he'd get his money back or take it out of Brian's hide.

Smith's always been a pain in the ass to us dealers, but he pays big money for big books so everyone tolerates him. He's a bit of a late payer though.'

'Do you know if Brian got paid for that six-figure book?' I asked Spears.

'I'm sure he did. Brian would never give up any book before he was fully paid. He would make sure he got his money before he ever gave Smith the book.'

'What was the book?'

'I don't know. Brian, like most book dealers liked to keep that information mum, especially during — and soon after — the initial stages of a sale.'

'Do you know anything about Brian's Value Book? I heard he kept a binder of all his valuable items with information on them in it,' I asked.

'No, not really, but I assume he kept such a book, many dealers — and even some collectors — do so. It helps if you keep accurate, precise records on all your holdings.'

5

Book Blasphemy

We left Alex Spears and headed out across town to the man who was said to be their chief competitor in the bookselling business, Andy Johns of Regal Books. In the car along the way Grant and I talked about what we'd just heard from Spears. I was actually surprised my new partner was so talkative but I guess the case was bugging him as much it was me, and he needed someone to sound off on about it.

'That guy, Spears, is a nut, Hollow,' Grant said simply. 'A freakin' nut!'

'Maybe.'

'No maybes about it! All those books, all them lousy cats, that damn smell. I thought I was gonna puke a dozen times. You know what? I think he did it. I think he murdered his partner.'

'Why do you say that? Not to get the

books. He wouldn't get them. He had to know that. The books would go to McDonald's wife, Milly.' I said casually, but then I wondered about it. 'Wouldn't they?'

'Would they?' Grant asked suspiciously.

That got me thinking and I thought about it for a while. Was there some sort of deal in the partnership? Maybe a secret will, or legal document, some contract that said Spears got all of McDonald's books upon his death? Maybe even vice versa? Could that be?

Probably not, I thought, but then again . . .

'So the partner is my chief suspect,' Grant stated as if he had finally solved everything — like the genius he was. 'Or maybe the wife? Maybe both?'

I shook my head in desperation, 'I don't know.'

'You don't know, Hollow! What the hell! What are you talking about?' Grant barked annoyed that I was not onboard with his brilliant theory.

'She was divorcing Brian, so she had a motive, I agree. She would have gotten half of the books — or the equivalent value in cash, anyway. So why kill him?'

'Greedy bitch, Hollow! Simple as that,' Grant said all-knowingly. 'Half wasn't good enough for her, she wanted it all.'

I nodded, 'That's possible, but I wonder if there is some contract regarding the books in the partnership.

'I never thought of that, Hollow,' he said, looking at me, still with disdain. 'I thought that old coot was hiding something. So maybe he is our boy after all?'

I didn't say anything about that. It was way too early for one thing, but mostly I didn't see Spears as a killer. Not the type at all. I liked the wife much more than the partner for the murder — but she had an airtight alibi. I decided to shelve all these thoughts for the moment and any further talk with Grant until we arrived at our next destination.

★ ★ ★

Andy Johns of Regal Books turned out to be a large fellow, actually quite obese, bald head, bad skin and a ruddy but smiling face. He smiled at us even when we told him we were cops. That surprised me and it got Grant suspicious right off.

Johns, unlike most of these book dealers, had an actual physical bookstore. In that regard, he seemed to be a rapidly diminishing breed, because from what I'd learned from Spears, independent book-stores would soon be a thing of the past. Like the dinosaurs. As well as the very idiosyncratic and independently-minded people who owned those stores. It was quite sad really, an important and even charming part of our culture was melting away to be lost forever.

Andy Johns lived in the small orderly apartment above his store. I assumed he owned the building, which was probably the only way he could afford to remain in business. He took us on a tour through the store, lined with rows of shelves of books. It was a well-ordered used book store that he told us also specialized in rare first editions that he proudly pointed to in a special group of glass display cases behind the front desk where the cash register was located. He was proud of his store, one of the last of the independents in our city and talked about its rich history since he'd founded it in 1974 when he was right out of college.

Johns led us to a stairway in the back, then upstairs, huffing and puffing all the way up each step. I feared he was going to have a heart attack right there at any moment and he was sweating profusely, even though it was far from warm. Once inside his apartment, I was surprised to see that there were very few books, only a couple of shelves in one common room. The rest of the place was as neat and orderly as Spears was messy. And not one cat was in evidence. Thank you, God!

'Those there' he said pointing to the only shelf with books upon it that I could see in the entire apartment, 'they're all sold. My online sales, the main part of my business these days. I have to package them up for mailing.'

Johns walked us into a small living room and over to some very comfortable-looking chairs. We sat down and got right down to it.

'So what do you guys want?' Johns

asked us, dropping himself slow-motion-like into a deep recliner with a heavy breath.

'You heard about Brian McDonald?' I began, looking for his reaction.

'Yeah, murdered they said on the TV news. I won't say I'm sorry, that bastard stole some of my best clients from me.'

'The way were heard it, *you* stole *his* best clients,' Grant countered sharply.

'Hah! So you been talking to Spears. That old guy is a total liar, you can't believe a damn word he says,' Johns replied hotly.

Charlie Grant and I looked at each other, I saw my detective partner roll his eyes in exasperation. I actually felt his pain. Almost.

'So who do you think killed Brian McDonald?' I asked Johns.

He laughed, 'It could be anyone.'

'Even you?' I asked bluntly.

He smiled but just shook his head no.

'So then, where were you when Brian was killed?' I asked.

'Oh no, it was not me.' Johns added quickly now that he thought he was becoming the focus of our efforts. 'I mean, it could be me. I hated the guy enough to do it, I guess — but no, I didn't kill Brian.'

'I suppose you have an alibi for the time of the murder?'

'I suppose I do,' he replied defiantly.

Grant and I were quiet for a moment. Waiting.

'Well, we'd really like to hear it, Mr. Johns,' I prompted.

'The night of the murder I had a book signing here. Two local authors and their fans, we launched their new books. *The Crossbow Murders*, the new one by Betty Flavory, latest in her Archery Murders series. Very hot! People getting killed with bows and arrows — a very modern setting. Great fun! Then I had Simon Kent here, he came out with a rather thin but sensationalized and unauthorized biography of that new pop star — Lady . . . what's her name? Anyway, the store was full of people and we had a nice wine and cheese book event all evening.'

'And you were here all evening and that can be verified?' I asked.

'Absolutely,' he replied simply. 'Where else would I go?'

I looked at him, that could be checked out easily enough later. 'So do you have any idea who killed Brian McDonald?'

'Well, my bet is on that crazy bastard, Alfred Smith. I mean, he was really hot to get his money back from Brian, from all I heard about it,' Johns told us almost *sotto voce*, like he was letting on to us some magical top secret in the book world. 'I sell to Smith too, he buys a lot of high-end pricey books. I hear he had some huge inheritance. He's a real octopus.'

'Octopus?' I asked curious. I'd never heard the term.

'Yeah, octopus, like in he's got eight hands and he uses them to make sure he gets to have everything. Got his hands in everywhere and on everything. A completist. But unlike everyone else, he's got the cash to actually be a true completist. Anyway, I heard that Brian screwed him on a big deal, almost half a million bucks.'

'For one freakin' book!' Grant blurted, he was shaking his head now. With what he'd heard about the value of that old Mormon book from Spears; now with this, Grant must have been thinking he was in the wrong profession.

So was I, I had to admit.

I let a wry grin play over my lips, knowing the collector field from my glass collecting, I knew it was not always that simple. Big dealer scores of high-value items with corresponding big money sales were not common. Most often, the item — whether book or glassware — will sit on a shelf unsold for months, if not years. The dealer ends up just tying up a lot of needed cash in an item that does not sell. Or he'd have to sell it at a loss to recoup his outlay. That would eat away any potential profit. It happened all the time. However, that rare big sale that came along from time to time really made up for it. It made it all worthwhile.

Johns looked over at Grant, 'Yes, from what I heard, it was some illuminated manuscript, something like that, something really rare. I think Brian stole it from some university library somewhere. You know, there's a lot of that sort of thing going on these days. It's all on the QT, of course. Or at least, a lot more of it is happening than people realize. I remember there was some guy in the Midwest, a really big case in the news a decade or so ago. He stole out of university libraries all the time. Thousands of books! Really valuable stuff. When the FBI raided his home they found it stuffed to the rafters with books, boxes of rare letters, manuscripts and more — almost all of it stolen. I think that's what Brian was into. That's the only way he could get the kind of rare, high-end, quality material to replenish his stock and be able to sell on such a regular basis.'

I looked from Johns to Grant, 'That puts an entirely different spin on this murder, if that's true.'

Grant shook his head, things were getting too complicated for him and he didn't like it.

I continued, 'If what you just told us is true about his stealing, how can we prove that? Where would he get the books from? I assume he wasn't doing the burglaries himself?'

Andy Johns shrugged, 'I'm an honest dealer and I run a legit store here. I sell books because I love books. You understand? I actually read them. I collect the ones I read, re-read the good ones. I also love turning readers onto new books that I have read and liked. It's a personal thing. From time to time I have people bring in a book or collection they want to sell to me and I know it *could* be stolen. I mean, I look at the item, then the sort of person who wants to sell it to me, and sometimes it just don't add up. You know? So it could be stolen. Or it could just be some kid selling grandpa's old books. Totally legit. That happens too. Who can really tell? I'm not in the FBI, I don't verify every buy. I do the best I can. Sometimes I buy it, sometimes not. I've rarely had anyone bring in the kind of high-end items Brian specialized in. I'm not hooked into selling to that high-end library and museum market, except for a few other customers I've cultivated over the years, which Brian has taken away from me now.'

'I see,' I said, afraid I was not really

seeing anything at all. I was wondering where we were going to find out about those stolen books. If this new branch of the case turned out to be true, it might give us a totally different reason for Brian McDonald's murder — and a totally different perp.

'I'm not hooked into the crooked end of the market, either,' Johns added sternly, showing his distaste. 'Maybe Al Spears would know, if you can get him to talk. Maybe Alfred Smith, the collector, would know. I'm sure his collector mania is sufficiently out of control to overcome any scruples he might have once had about buying stolen books. To me, and most honest dealers and collectors, such theft is not only a crime, it's blasphemy. Blasphemy against books and the entire field.'

'Blasphemy?' Grant asked with a grin.

'Yep, that's how a lot of us feel,' Johns said seriously, his eyes sharply looking at Grant. 'Of course, that wouldn't play with a guy like Brian McDonald though, and I'm sure Spears and Smith are the same way. Well, maybe not Spears. I'm not crazy about him, but I guess he is honest. I do have to admit it. We just don't get along — mostly Brian's fault — him being Brian's partner for so long. Hell, Maybe Brian, Spears and Smith were in this all together? Like some secret conspiracy?'

'A book conspiracy?' I asked mildly curious.

'Yes, that's it, a damn conspiracy!' Johns replied almost dreamily. 'A real biblio-murder conspiracy!'

Grant just shook his head, muttered under his breath, 'They're all freakin' nuts!'

'Thanks for your time, Mr. Johns,' I said, then Grant and I got out of there fast.

'So what's next on the list?' Grant asked me once we were in the car and set to drive away from Andy Johns store.

'We have to talk to that collector, Fred Smith, then maybe Brian's mistress, Alice Larkin — and maybe even that former maid, the one he had a dalliance with, Angela Hedger,' I told him.

'Just three more to go, and we're still

no closer to closing this murder,' Grant said impatiently. 'You know what I think? I like the partner for this. Thing is, we have to check to find out who gets the books after Brian's death — the wife, or the partner?'

'Then let's go back and see Spears about that,' I said, hoping we'd get down to the bottom of that question. I also wanted to find out what Spears knew about Brian's theft of books from university libraries. There seemed something much deeper there that needed to be brought out to the light of day.

Grant shrugged, having no better idea, 'All right, let's do that.'

6

Mysterious Sources

Al Spears was not happy to see us again and his face showed it, but our faces showed him that we were not happy with his bullshit story of a few hours earlier. That had told us nothing and sent us on our way knowing less than when we'd first gotten there.

'Murder's a serious charge, Mr. Spears,' I told him flatly, laying it out. 'Your story doesn't add up. Care to explain it?'

'Explain what?' he stammered, growing concerned now.

'You told us Andy Johns stole Brian's best clients — Johns told us Brian stole his clients. Now which is it?'

Spears laughed mildly, the tension melting off his face. 'Oh, that's all you wanted to know? Look, Detectives, everyone steals clients and contacts from each other in this business. We all buy and sell, and then resell, to each other all the time. This field is more incestuous than a hillbilly whorehouse.'

Grant shook his head in annoyance. I could see that he didn't buy Spears' explanation, but I was a collector and I knew collectors. What he said seemed valid to me. However, I had something else on my mind that I wanted to put to Spears but Grant spoke up before I could get it out.

'What about that Value Book?' Grant asked sharply, looking at Spears intently, daring him to lie. 'You knew about that?'

'I never saw it, but I assume Brian had some type of book to keep records. We all do. I mean, we all have something; a book, a printout or a database on a computer, something to keep records of our stock and prices. Brian didn't use a computer, so he didn't even have a printout, so he had to have some kind of hand-written record book, but like I say, I never saw it,' he said simply.

I nodded, that seemed to fit. Even Grant seemed to acknowledge what Spears said, though reluctantly.

Now to the real reason we'd come back here to see Spears. I said, 'Tell us, who gets McDonald's books now? He's dead, so who inherits them? You, or the widow?'

Spears looked mildly surprised by my question, 'Why, the widow, she gets them all, of course. What would ever make you think otherwise?'

'Are you sure?' Grant asked acidly, suspicious as ever. 'Maybe you and McDonald had some kind of secret business agreement or hidden contract, some letter of understanding? Maybe there is something in his will? Tell me now. We will check this out, Spears, and if you're lying to us . . . '

'Being honest with us now,' I added, 'will go a long way to keeping you off the suspect list. It's a list you do not want to be on, let me tell you. You can't sell books from prison.'

Spears looked at me seriously. Shocked. He brushed away Edgar Allan Poe. The cat meowed and ran out of the room as if highly insulted.

'They won't even let you have any books in prison. Well, maybe one or two paperbacks, but not a fine collection like this — and no cats either,' I added, sealing the deal.

Spears gulped nervously at that last remark, which really seemed to get his attention. 'No, I'm telling you, Milly gets it all, I am sure. That's why Brian and I had our books separate in our homes, instead of in one central location. That way no wife, no family, would get all our stock in the event of a death or the break-up of our business.'

'We'll check that, Spears, so you better be telling us the truth,' Grant growled, giving the man a touch of his bad-cop routine, though he seemed mollified for now. He was probably already figuring another angle on the murder and making the wife for the killer.

'Detective, I am telling you the truth. I swear.'

I looked over at Spears, he was relaxing, he was calming down.

Now I was ready to get to the real reason for *my* visit and why *I* wanted to talk to him again.

'Where did Brian get all those quality,

high-end books he sold for such big money?' I asked Spears.

'I don't know. I assume he bought them on the market, like we all do. From other collectors, estate sales. Also probably from the Internet,' he said simply, but I could see he was uncomfortable talking about this and it was obvious he was hiding something.

'Really? You and Brian weren't involved in any crooked dealings, selling stolen high-end books, maybe stolen from college or university libraries?' I asked more forcefully.

I could see Spears become uncomfortable, growing nervous

'He's holding back,' Grant said with a snarl. He could smell deception, even through the cat odour that permeated the house.

'Mr. Hollow . . . '

'Detective Hollow,' I corrected sharply.

'Detective Hollow,' Spears said nervously, careful now. 'Do not link me with anything Brian may have done. Please. I did not know Brian's intimate business, just some snippets of what he told me; the usual woman trouble with his wife, things like that, some rumours in the trade about other dealers or collectors. But you are right, he did seem to come across an unusual amount of quality books and ephemera that he sold for big money. It was really quite amazing. I have to admit I was jealous about his sources. They were good. Almost too good.'

'He ever tell you where he got any of these books?' I continued.

'No, and that in and of itself doesn't mean much. All dealers guard their sources and contacts most jealously. They do not divulge them, especially not to another dealer. A competitor. Sources and contacts are the lifeblood of our business and of our success.'

I nodded, being a collector myself, I knew what Spears was saying was true. The collectable glassware field, especially with Depression Glass was very competitive and sources and contacts were guarded like gold.

'Okay, I'll buy that now — up to a point,' I prompted, because I could see there was something on Spears' mind.

Something just wasn't sitting well with him. 'I see you're holding back. What is it?'

'I don't know, Detective Hollow,' Spears said carefully, 'I don't know. There's something that I always wondered about regarding Brian's business. Brian came across some incredible items — truly amazing — books and ephemera that are hardly ever seen on the open market these days. It was not anything that would draw attention from the news media, he wasn't selling the *Madrid Codex* or Guttenberg *Bibles* wholesale, nothing like that, just items that you saw once every ten or twenty years. And there was just too much of it. I mean, it was like he had a secret vault somewhere or a time machine where he was able to get the stuff, or maybe he was buying it . . . on the Black Market.'

'A Black Market in books?' Grant asked surprised. He gave me a look like now he'd heard it all.

'A Black Market in *rare* books, yes . . . and in famous author letters, manuscripts, and other valuable ephemera, most definitely.' Spears explained simply. 'Then there are illuminated manuscripts, rare Dark Age volumes hand copied by Irish monks in the 12th Century, papyrus scrolls — not the Dead Sea Scrolls, mind, but almost as old — ancient Roman and Greek texts . . . You get it? Anyway, Brian seemed to find it all and sold it all. I believe his biggest buyers were not the type of collectors I and most of my brethren sell to at all. Brian sold to large institutional collections, mostly university and college libraries, museums and the like. Some rich foreign collectors, too.'

I looked at Spears and smiled, asking incredulously, 'Are you telling me that the same institutions and libraries Brian sold to — were the same ones he was stealing from?'

Spears gulped nervously, grinned sheepishly, 'I never thought of it that way. I don't really know. It could be possible. Many of these large institutions have no idea of their holdings — other than the one or two privileged authors or popular collections they hold close and dear. Everything else is usually stored in cardboard boxes piled off in some corner of some basement building never even having been opened and examined since it was first given to the library. No one knows. No one cares. I hesitate to say this, but in some cases Brian might have even been doing the world a favour by making this material available to collectors again — to those who truly cherish these items. Rather than have them lay in a box in a room for years, or decades, in some cold, mouldy basement, slowly being damaged by insects — or worse, destroyed by a fire or flood and lost to us forever. It happens, Detectives, it happens all too often. I'm not approving of this, like I say, but I understand it. Regardless, I have no real evidence of just what Brian was up to, only a gut feeling that I did not want to think about. It is as simple as this. Something was not right in the way Brian was selling books.'

I digested all this before I spoke, looked over at Grant, who just looked bored. Well, there'd be no help from him.

'Would Brian's lost Value Book have all this data in it? Including where he got the book originally and the cost?' I asked Spears.

'It may, it should, it could. Like I say,

I've never seen this book, but perhaps,' Spears replied.

I looked at Grant and he shrugged, 'Coulda, woulda, shoulda . . . ' was all he said.

'Am I a suspect, Detective?' Spears asked me cautiously. Gone now was the frivolity of hours before exhibited by him upon our first visit. Now at the thought of being charged with his partner's murder Spears was seriously concerned. Even afraid.

I wasn't buying Spears as our killer, but I knew Grant had a bias for the fellow. Then there was also the wife. I guess Grant was putting two and two together and coming up with five, or seven, or whatever as usual, and figuring out which one of them would fit best to close the case. He never asked me nor cared what I thought, he just wanted the case closed so it would all go away.

'If you were being charged, Spears, we'd cuff you and bring your ass in right now,' Grant said with a twisted grimace. 'What we want is information on the killer.'

'I want to know about how and where

McDonald got those books. Who was he partnered with?' I asked Spears, who looked at me with alarm since he was McDonald's partner and thought he would somehow be implicated in something nefarious. 'I mean, who was he partnered with in these book thefts? Who was stealing the books for him?'

Spears though about that for a moment and eventually shook his head in consternation. 'There's not many book people — dealers or collectors — who would ever consider such a thing. In the book world, it's looked upon as . . . a kind of . . . '

'Blasphemy?' I supplied the term Spears had been looking for, which I remembered Andy Johns using with us earlier.

'Yes, correct . . . it is book blasphemy . . . it is blasphemy against books, against knowledge, which is what we all prize most,' Spears said dead serious now.

Grant laughed at that, insultingly nasty.

Spears just sighed, adding, 'I admit there is the odd crook here and there when it comes to stretching the rules of selling, or taking advantage of a client, but out and out burglary? And of a library?' — he said the word 'library' like it was absolutely sacred. 'No, Detective, I know of no one, nor could I think of anyone, who would ever do such a thing.'

'Yeah, well, what about that collector freak, Fred Smith, that we heard about?' Grant asked quickly. 'He seems greedy enough.'

Spears gave us a mild laugh, 'Fred is a dear friend, but a murderer? Never! However, you are right about him being greedy, he's greedy for books, or at least greedy for the books he wants. But he would never do anything to put his collection in jeopardy, or do anything that might separate him from it. Like something that could get him jail time. You have to understand him, like I do. He loves his books — better than he does people. Yes, he would buy a stolen item — no one ever asks any questions about that, and I'm sure he has some stolen items in his collection — either known or unknown. But would he go into a university library, pretend to be doing specialized research, sign in under his own ID — or even worse, a fake ID — to access a special collection with the thought of theft? Never. Would he kill Brian McDonald? Impossible!'

I sighed, Grant just hit his fist upon the table. I knew he felt like his best bet had just busted out. I looked at Grant and he had a blank look on his face. This was getting to him. Well, screw him, I thought.

'I've had enough of books and book people,' Grant growled finally, ending his sentence with a curse, which could have been at Spears, or me, or books in general. I figured it was at me, because he was looking at me when he said it. 'So what now, Hollow?'

I shrugged. What now, indeed?

I looked back to Spears. 'Look, if Brian was stealing rare books and other stuff from university libraries and special collections, it would have to be through someone who knew rare books. Someone who knew what to look for, what to take, right?'

'Of course,' he said simply, but then he explained, 'Your average criminal, any

99

B&E guy, even a top cat burglar — remember I specialize in selling crime fiction and true crime — would never even consider mere 'books.' They want money, or gold coins or jewellery, stuff they can turn into cash right away. Certainly not books! No, if Brian was stealing books for resale, he was doing it all by himself. Remember, these are prized books in special collections, locked cases, locked rooms even, and you have to sign-in to view them and handle them. You must show identification and have legitimate credentials as a scholar, journalist or collector doing serious research.'

I nodded, Spears had a point. It wasn't any conspiracy or gang of book thieves. Brian McDonald was doing the thefts all by himself and it should be easy enough to find out for sure how he did it. On our way out I told Spears to make a list of places for us to contact. I told him I'd call him first thing tomorrow morning for the list.

★   ★   ★

When we left Spears' residence I told Charlie Grant my plan. He wasn't happy about it. It would mean a lot of phone work tomorrow morning, which he hated, but he admitted he didn't have any better ideas and that it might yield some results.

'Look, today's shot. Early tomorrow I'll call Spears and get that list from him of ten local libraries that have the kind of stuff McDonald was selling. Then we'll check their records to see if McDonald had ever signed-in to access any of their collections. Then we'll have him!'

Grant looked at me with a scrunched up face. 'Look, Hollow, I'll go along with this but I can't see how it gets us any closer to finding McDonald's murderer. So he was stealing rare books? So what?'

'Maybe someone found out about it?' I proposed, trying to whet his interest.

Grant just looked at me and laughed. He laughed at me and maybe he was right. It was a long shot. It wasn't like Brian McDonald had a partner doing the stealing with him — or for him. And I didn't buy the notion that Spears was involved. Even Grant seemed to have dropped that idea now and seemed to be concentrating on the wife, Milly.

'So where does that leave us?' I asked him.

'In the soft stuff,' Grant shot back quickly.

I nodded. 'I'll see you in the squad room tomorrow morning.'

'Whatever.'

7

Identity Theft

The next day was the third day after Brian McDonald's murder and I was no closer to finding his murderer than I had been when Captain Wallace had first paired me up with Charlie Grant. That had proved to be a cop partnership created in hell, but I knew I'd have to make the best of it. Worse than that even, I had to make it work, and that meant finding the killer and closing the case. Otherwise I was sure Captain Wallace would take any failure out of my own hide.

When I walked into the squad room that morning I saw Grant was already in with Captain Wallace. The office door was closed and they were talking rather animatedly. I could imagine what the topic was, and it wasn't the McDonald murder — or perhaps only peripherally. I walked over to the end of the room and when they noticed me approaching the office Grant opened the door and walked out. He came straight over to me.

'I just wanted to tell you, Hollow,' Grant stated with maximum sarcasm dripping from his voice, 'I asked Cap to take me off this damn case. You've made a mess of it. I told him because of you, it will go cold case by the end of the week. He didn't like that. Now you've got us looking for stolen books? I asked him to split us up as partners. I told him you're a freakin' nut case and that I want out.'

We were quiet for a long moment after that, just glaring at each other.

Then I realized something, Grant hadn't lowered the boom. I smiled, told him with a snicker, 'So I guess we're still partners and you're still on the case.'

Grant's face grew beet red and he strode away from me almost apoplectic. When he was a few feet away I heard him shout, 'Asshole!'

'Moron!' I barked back loudly.

The entire squad room looked at him and then over to me. Some of the guys laughed. Others clapped. They loved good cop-type entertainment.

I sighed, what the hell could I say to top that?

I went over to my desk and sat down, tried to calm myself and then placed a call to Al Spears. He was up and waiting for my call, ready with the list and he gave it to me over the phone. I quickly wrote it down. He'd been thorough, not only giving me the names of ten local university libraries and special collections that were excellent prospects, but he also included the name of a contact person at each location and their phone number.

'Thanks, Mr. Spears,' I said, surprised by his depth of cooperation, 'this is a big help.'

'No problem, you'd be amazed what you can do on Google and the Internet. Good luck, and let me know how it all turns out.'

I thanked him again, then hung up the phone. I cut the list in half and then called over Charlie Grant.

'What the hell you want now, Hollow?'

I gave him his half of Spears' list. 'Here,

make the calls on these five. I'll call the other five.'

'So what are we looking for?' he grumbled.

'We want to know if Brian McDonald signed-in to get access to any of these special collections.'

'I know that, idiot! I mean, so what does it mean if we find anything? Why are we doing this?'

I looked at Charlie Grant hard. I didn't want to reach over my desk and bitch slap him into a stupor — I mean, actually I did — but I'd have to cool it with that type of thinking for now. Instead I told him, 'Just do it, then we'll go on from there.'

'Whatever.'

We made the calls.

It took a lot longer than either of us ever thought it would. Going through college and university bureaucracy, even in the library field, turned out to be just unbelievable. I called and spoke to a bunch of overly academic guys and gals, all anal retentive types, dourly officious and ultimately annoying to the point of making me want to scream at their blockheadedness. Over-educated idiots. I mean, did these people take stupid pills? Finally I was able to get them to clue into the fact that I was investigating a murder and asked about the sign-in sheets and Brian McDonald's name. They gave me endless rigamarole about privacy considerations and rules so I had to take them through the entire process, then go through their supervisors. I got the feeling none of them really liked cops at all. When any info was able to be pried from their cold bureaucratic academician fingers, I came up empty for a lead. That left me dead in the water.

I reluctantly walked around my desk to where Charlie Grant sat at his desk making calls, 'Anything on your five with McDonald?'

'No. Nothing,' he said flatly. 'They never heard of him.'

'Really?'

'Yeah, none of them ever heard of any Brian McDonald. His name is not on any of their sign-in sheets.'

That just didn't ring true. I looked at

Grant and he looked back at me with a wicked told-you-so sneer, happy my little plan had sunk faster than the *Titanic*.

'What now, genius?'

What now, indeed?

I stood there a moment thinking, or trying to think. Finally I said, 'Look, Brian McDonald was definitely going into these libraries to steal stuff, just like that ex-Clinton official Sandy Berger. Remember him? He was convicted of stealing a lot of top-secret presidential documents from the National Archives, all stashed in his pants and socks.'

'Yeah, Sandy *Burglar*. I remember him.'

'Anyway, if someone could do it with presidential papers at the National Archives in Washington D.C., it wouldn't be much of a stretch for Brian McDonald to do it at some understaffed libraries here in the city,' I offered.

'So?' was Grant's only reply.

I looked at him closely, he was being no help at all. I could see he didn't give a damn about helping me or working the case — he wanted off it in the worse way.

I knew I'd have to play this almost all on my own. So be it. No sweat really, maybe it was better that way.

'Look, I'm going to call my five names again, get their fax number and send them that photo of McDonald we got from his wife. Then we'll see if anyone remembers him. You call back your five and do the same thing, okay?'

'All right, Hollow, I'll try that. One more time, then that's it. Maybe he used an alias or an assumed name.'

'He used something,' I said.

Then we got to work, made the calls again, explained everything all over again, then faxed over the photo to the contacts Spears had given us at the ten libraries.

Then we waited.

An hour later I got the first call back from the Wilson University Library. Director Harold Crowhank whined into my ear, 'Yes, I recognize the photo, Detective. He has been here on numerous occasions but not under the name you gave us, not under Brian McDonald. Oh no, not under that name at all. We have no listing for him under Brian McDonald.'

'Then what name do you have him listed under?' I asked sharply, impatient now and chomping at the bit for a break. I knew this might be the break we were looking for.

'I'll have to ask the staff,' Crowhank said thoughtfully, 'you see, they do most of the grunt work here.'

'Don't they check ID's?' I chided.

'Of course they do, but you have to understand these are, for the most part, pimple-faced freshmen trying to earn a few bucks at a scud work job. Or simply volunteers. They don't run the library or investigate IDs. They look at a driver's licence, see if the photo matches the person with the ID, then take down the name. They're not the FBI, they can't tell if an ID is fake or not, and we don't want them to do that. We don't want to inconvenience our visitors, many of whom are influential people in the media or scholars doing important research.'

'I see,' I said softly. 'No wonder so much stuff is being stolen.'

Crowhank picked up on that at once, I could feel the tension in his voice,

'Stolen? Are you telling me the library has been the victim of a theft in one of its rare papers collections?'

'Nothing we can prove yet, sir, so calm down, please,' I said. 'Just talk to your staff and get back to me as soon as you can about the name that goes with that photo.'

'I will do that right away,' Crowhank said, then hung up.

I checked with Charlie Grant next. He was having some trouble, waiting for people to get back to him who were slow in responding. It set him off.

It was near noon, Grant was getting antsy and got up from his desk and just walked away towards the large double doors at the end of the squad room.

'Hey?' I shouted. 'Where you going?'

'If you must know, I'm going to lunch,' he said coldly.

'You could let me know,' I told him.

'I don't have to clear anything with you, Hollow, remember that,' he said sharply, then he walked out of the squad room in a huff.

I fell back into my chair with a groan,

staring at the phone, willing it to ring, but it was as dead as my chances of any promotion in this department. Some of the guys had ordered in and I had them get me a hero, then I got a coke from the machine in the hallway. It was a quiet meal, I sat alone at my desk, trying to figure this case out and coming up empty.

Then the phone on my desk started ringing. The phone on Grant's desk also started ringing.

I picked up my phone right away; it was Crowhank. 'Detective, Hollow?'

'Yes, sir,' I said trying to keep calm, hoping this might be the break I needed.

'Detective Hollow, we had a match. One of our second year students put the face to a name.'

'Not Brian McDonald?' I asked hopefully.

'Oh no, not at all. Get this, he told me the name used was Alex Spears,' Crowhank said proudly, like he was enjoying being my own personal junior G-Man.

Alex Spears? I shook my head, either Spears had been playing us all along — which I could not believe — or Brian

McDonald was a lot more cunning than I'd given him credit for. This didn't look good. Spears could be a dead end.

I looked up as I saw Charlie Grant come over to his desk and pick up his ringing phone. He started talking to the caller. I tried to hear what was being said, wondering if it was some news we needed.

'Detective?' Crowhank asked, getting my attention back to his call. 'Are you still there?'

'Oh . . . yes, of course, Mr. Crowhank, I'm right here. Just thinking.'

'Well, I hope this has been of help to you. Are you sure there has been no theft in my library?' he asked, which I realized was his main and only concern now.

'Honestly, we don't know yet.'

'That sounds bad,' he said, his voice tense, nervous.

'I won't sugar-coat it for you. We're looking into things but we just started. This is just a sidebar on a murder investigation. I'll let you know if anything comes of it,' I told him. I wanted to get off the phone and see what Grant had come up with — if anything.

'A sidebar? The Wilson Library is not just a sidebar, Detective, even in a murder case. It's an important institution of higher learning to our city, to our nation, a repository of some of the most priceless collections of letters and papers written by major authors, scientists and politicians — the movers and shakers of our nation for the last one hundred years!'

I sighed, he was certainly correct, but I had nothing to tell him now and I wanted to cut the call. 'As soon as I find out anything, Mr. Crowhank, I'll let you know.'

The other end of the phone went silent for a moment, then Crowhank said, 'I'll hold you to that, Detective,' then he hung up.

I shook my head in exasperation, put Crowhank and his problems out of my mind and concentrated on Brian McDonald. So McDonald had been using the name of his partner Alex Spears? He had a fake ID, probably a driver's licence with Spears' name on it but with his own photo, something that looked good enough to get past some college kid with the attention span of a gnat. So, was McDonald just using the fake ID, or was he planning on framing Spears if the thefts were ever discovered? I thought about that and realized it was most likely both. McDonald was a cunning bastard. No wonder he had been murdered.

I got out of my chair and walked around my desk towards Grant. He was off the phone now and I told him what Crowhank had told me.

'Yeah, what I just heard jibes with that, Hollow. The guy at Cornell Library Special Collections, told me the photo definitely matched a man who kept coming in to examine certain author collections. The name was Alex Spears.'

I nodded, 'But it wasn't Spears, it was McDonald.'

'Yeah, so Spears is in the clear, I guess,' Grant admitted reluctantly. 'This Brian McDonald was a sharpie all right, using his partner's name like that, but I can see the smarts behind it. Every time I get a room with a hooker I sign in under the name Bentley Hollow,' he laughed wickedly.

'Nice one,' I said, wondering if he was telling me the truth.

'So now what? I mean, knowing McDonald stole rare books for resale tells us he was a crook and a weasel, but it doesn't get us one inch closer to his killer,' Grant stated.

I had to admit it, my square head partner had a point there.

I had another plan I'd been formulating while I'd been on the phone, so I told it to Grant now.

'Listen, I think it's time we split up. Why don't you go back and speak to the wife about the books and see who gets them now that McDonald's dead. It should be her. If you have time left, maybe run by the ex-maid — McDonald was caught doing her by the wife — then maybe pay the mistress a visit? She might know something.'

Grant smiled, I knew he'd jump at the female bait I was putting out there to get him out of my hair. 'Yeah, okay, I been curious about all these women all along — see if they're as hot as McDonald thought.'

I shrugged, 'Whatever.'

'What about you, Hollow?' he asked suspicion suddenly clouding his face.

'I'm going back to talk with Spears again, see if I can find out why McDonald used his name to sign-in and what his reaction is to that. I don't think he's the killer but he may know more than he is letting on. I also want to see if he ever did research himself at any of the ten libraries he gave us. He seemed to have a lot of information on them, like he'd been there before. Makes me wonder. Then I'm going to talk to that ex-wife again.'

'The lezbo?' Grant laughed, giving me a throat-cutting gesture.

'Yeah.'

'Well, you won't get nothing from her, I tried. If I couldn't melt her you won't have a ghost of a chance. She probably hates men. They all do.'

I wondered why. 'Thanks for your concern.'

'Just trying to set you straight, Hollow. Get it? Straight? You're barking up the wrong tree.'

'I'm not barking up any tree, Grant,

she's a witness, that's all.'

'Yeah, sure,' he laughed. 'I'll see you back here tomorrow morning.'

'Tomorrow morning,' I said as I walked away.

I couldn't get away from Charlie Grant soon enough. Now I was on my own, Grant was doing his thing and I was doing my own thing, and that's the way I liked it. It was good to not have to look at his beady little eyes and see that smart-aleck look on his face.

8

Surprise Visitor

I didn't think we'd get much from Grant's visit with any of the three women he had agreed to talk to. I just wanted him to do something he thought might be useful — or better yet, just fun — anything that got him out of my hair. The wife, Milly McDonald was a pretty straight-ahead greedy bitch looking for a large cash payday on her husband's left behind books — their cash value, that is. The two other women McDonald had had affairs with — the maid and the mistress — I didn't expect much from them either. Then again, you never knew. I wanted to remain hopeful. I'd just have to wait and see what Grant dug up, if anything. Meanwhile, I'd go my own way, and that's the way I liked it.

I spent the rest of the morning with Brian McDonald's partner, Alex Spears, at his home, talking about Brian, books, and the ins and outs of the book business — in between the cats. The cat smell hadn't abated since I'd been there last. I tried to put all that out of my mind as I concentrated on business.

'Back again,' Spears said carefully as he greeted me at the door to his house. 'You're not here to arrest me, are you?'

I laughed, 'No, Mr. Spears. First off, I want to thank you for the library leads you gave me.'

'No problem, Detective Hollow,' he said. 'Did they pan out for you?'

'Yes, actually, they did.'

He smiled, a bit excited that he was able to help the cops in a real murder investigation. He was a crime fiction reader and true crime buff and it was coming through now in his reaction to my news. 'Well then, by all means come in. You must tell me all about it.'

So I told him all about it and it didn't make him happy at all. In fact, he was in an uproar of righteous indignation, and then sudden worry. 'My God! My good name will be ruined, my business ruined!

How could Brian do such a thing?'

'McDonald didn't want to use his own name to sign-in, that would prove he had been to each of these libraries — and who knows how many more?' I offered.

'Oh, my, it's even worse that I thought then. Brian travelled extensively. He may have been doing these thefts all across the country. I am most distressed to hear this news, Detective Hollow. He used my good name, my own good name!' Spears was absolutely beside himself with trepidation and I tried to calm him and get him to focus on talking about McDonald and the book business. It took me a while. I had to impress upon him there would be no liability or criminal charges against him because McDonald had used his name fraudulently.

'You're the victim here,' I told Spears. 'What happened to you was essentially identity theft. You cannot be held accountable for what Brian did.'

Spears sighed, breathing deeply, obviously much relieved but still quite concerned. 'That bastard! That son-of-a-bitch! He not only stole from our business, he stole rare library books and he stole my identity! I tell you, Detective Hollow, with what I know now, if Brian McDonald wasn't already dead, I'd kill him myself!'

I wasn't shocked by his words.

Spears looked at me sheepishly, 'I hope nothing I tell you here can be used against me, Detective.'

'Don't worry about it,' I told him, as I looked around the room at the shelves full of books. 'Why don't you tell me about these? The books. What makes them so special, so valuable?'

Spear quickly brightened, 'Why, Detective Hollow, I'd be happy to. I could see you have an interest in collecting, but knew it was not books.'

'No, not books, Depression Glassware,' I said.

'Ah, yes, Jadite, Fenton, Carnival and such?'

'Yes, but I'm getting interested in books. Can you teach me about them?' I prompted.

'That's a tall order. There's so much to tell,' Spears began but with obvious enthusiasm. 'I mean, books are wonder-ful, endlessly fascinating. Take a look at some of the ones I have here on the shelves. Go ahead, pull one out, take a look.'

I did as he said. I looked over the bound edges of the books that were facing me on the shelves, what I had learned was called the spine of the book. These spines showed the names of titles and authors. Some of the names I recognized. I saw a copy of James M. Cain's *The Postman Always Rings Twice* and pulled it out. 'I remember the movie with Lana Turner and John Garfield.'

'Yeah, she was a real peach in her day. The film was from 1946. That book is the first edition, from Knopf in 1934. It's lightly cocked, but otherwise in fine condition, you picked a good book.'

'Did I?' I asked, showing my surprise. I had no idea.

'Yes, the jacket is what makes it, it's in lovely condition. I value it at about $6,000. I have a buyer, or at least, someone seriously interested. Another dealer, drat! If I resell it to him, I'll have to give him the standard 20 percent discount to the trade. I'd rather sell it to a collector at the full price but maybe it is time for it to go.'

'I see.' I looked the book over. The jacket didn't seem to be much, just some fancy lettering of the title with smaller letters at the lower edge of the author's name. I put it back on the shelf. Then I reached over and picked up a small book that was near it, a paperback, a very old paperback.

'That's interesting, do you know what you have there?'

I shrugged, 'I haven't the faintest idea. *The Good Earth* by Pearl Buck, right?'

Spears laughed, genuinely happy to talk books and I had to admit his enthusiasm was getting to me, 'Yes, but it is a very special book. Actually it is an historical artifact, an icon of American publishing.'

'Really?' I was interested but sceptical. I mean, it was just a paperback.

'That's because it's the very *first* mass-market paperback ever. In 1939 Simon & Schuster partnered with Robert de Graff to publish Pocket Books, which began the Paperback Revolution, which spread like wildfire across the country, and then across the world. All Pocket Books were numbered. The number run reached over a thousand, much higher even. Look at the spine. Do you see any number?'

I turned the book and looked at the bound edge, the spine. 'No, there's no number.'

'That's right!' Spears almost shouted in his excitement. 'In 1939 Pocket Books published a tiny trial edition of that book with no number, only 2,000 copies that were given away to influential persons, and distributed only in New York City. There are less than a dozen copies known to exist today.'

'What's the value of something like that?' I asked, not very impressed. I mean, it didn't look like much of a book to me. And it was just a paperback. I didn't think paperbacks were worth anything. Coupla dollars, maybe?

'Well, it is worth perhaps $5,000. It's a very nice copy,' Spears said with a smile at my evident surprise.

I carefully put it back on his shelf.

'That much, for just a paperback?'

'Oh, yes, and you'd be surprised to know that many paperbacks go for big money these days. Not as much as hardcover firsts of course, but in the hundreds of dollars and sometimes in the thousands of dollars. There is a very frantic market for certain paperbacks. You know about first editions?'

'Yes, that is the first time a book has appeared in print, right?' I answered carefully. At that point I wasn't so sure of what I knew and something told me the old guy was going to throw me a curve.

'Correct, but many collectable authors, many famous books, originally appeared in paperback. These are called, appropriately enough, paperback originals. These paperbacks are the first true editions. Many famous genre writers got their start in the forties, fifties and sixties in paperback, so you'll find a lot of key mystery, crime, science fiction and horror work that originally appeared in paperback. These are avidly collected by fans. Paperbacks also have better cover art than hardcover books, much more sexy, passionate, violent, much more exciting overall — and that's exciting to collectors. There are even books published that reproduce the best paperback cover art. The artists have their own followings too.'

I sighed, I had a lot to learn. I looked over at the shelves again. 'You have some very expensive books here.'

'Yes, but these books did not just appear one day, mysteriously. They are the result of a lifetime of collecting, a lifetime in books, my friend. I buy everywhere I can, I search constantly, it is fun, part of the joy of collecting. The hunt!'

'I know that feeling.'

'I am sure you do, from your glass collecting, certainly. Well, I hunt and buy from other dealer lists, book shows, yard sales, flea markets, thrift stores, and the best when I can get them, estate sales. It is great fun and gives me much joy, and it has given me a decent living doing something I love. What can be better?'

I noticed another book and pulled it down to look at it more closely.

'Ah, yes, the Steinbeck, that's a very

nice copy. It took me a lot of work to get that one. I got it from an old collector who bought it new when it first came out in 1939. It was a real job to get him to part with it and I think I overpaid, but I'm not bothered by that now. It's in lovely condition, a hint of foxing, but the jacket is glorious, so I am well pleased with it.'

'*The Grapes of Wrath*,' I said, looking over the jacket art showing Oakie farmers during the Depression. What's something like this worth?'

'I conservatively estimate it at $20,000.'

I grimaced and put the book back on the shelf. 'This is a bit overwhelming.'

Spears laughed, 'It can be, there is a lot to learn, a lot to know. I've been in the business for over 30 years and every day I learn something new. The important thing as a dealer is that selling books is my bread and butter, so I don't want to get caught with my pants down.'

I smiled, 'What do you mean?'

'No one can know everything. Smarties abound, but always get outsmarted. Every dealer has their interests and specialty, but when they come across something outside that realm they can become nervous, they have to be careful.'

'I know what you mean you can sell too cheap if you don't know what you have. It's the same with glassware,' I said, remembering the competitiveness there for prime pieces among dealers.

'Correct. It can be a bit of a crap shoot, but a pleasant one. I could think of no other way to spend my time on this old world of ours,' Spears said softly, thoughtful now. 'But what do you like to read? Do you have a favourite book, a favorite author?'

I sighed, 'Police work doesn't give me much time for reading. I like private eye stories, Dashiell Hammett, Raymond Chandler, crime fiction generally, and some science fiction and horror.'

'Hammett, Chandler, probably Stephen King, perhaps in science fiction, Isaac Asimov?'

'Yeah, he wrote *The Foundation Trilogy*, didn't he? I read them in school.'

Al Spears got up and walked over to the shelf behind him, pulling down three hardcover books wrapped in clear shiny plastic. 'Here they are, Asimov's Foundation Trilogy; *Foundation, Foundation and Empire* and *Second Foundation.*'

He handed me the books and I looked at the jacket art. They showed spaceships and alien faces. They were lovely and the condition was really nice, almost like new. 'These must be old. I remember these covers from when I was a kid, from the high school library.'

'Not these books, Detective Hollow, but ones just like them, reprints certainly, or book club editions, which abound. These are the first editions from Gnome Press, a small science fiction specialty publisher. They were published one each year, from 1951 to 1953 and these copies have the added bonus of being signed by the author.'

'Do signed books bring a higher price?' I asked.

'Good question. That depends on the author. Asimov did sign quite a bit. Other authors don't sign much, some won't. Others, sadly, die young. Unfortunately, the signature on most books contributes little if nothing to its overall value.'

'So Asimov signed these? Are they worth more signed.'

'For Asimov absolutely. You see, while Asimov signed a lot of books, he is a revered science fiction writer, a real icon, and these three books are his magnum opus. You know, he also wrote sequels back in the '80s and the '90s before he died, later other writers continued the series, but these three were the originals. There is significant demand. They are science fiction cornerstones as well. I'd place them easily at $5,000 a piece, perhaps as much as $20,000 for the set of three.'

'Wow!' I blurted, in spite of myself. It was amazing, the world of rare books was like an entire new world that had suddenly opened up before me. I was just glad that Charlie Grant wasn't here. My moron partner would just be annoyed by all this book talk, and I didn't want anything to interfere with my newly acquired fascination for books. I carefully handed Spears back his Asimovs.

'Nice, eh?' he asked me with a glint to his eyes as he took the books and placed them back on his shelf.

'Yeah, but nothing I can afford.'

Spears nodded sagely, 'Yes, that is true for now, but not always, and there are great finds still out there. All you have to do is look. You'd be surprised. You just have to know what to look for.'

'That's just it, I don't know what to look for.'

Spears smiled, 'Yes you do, you have an advisor.'

'I do?'

'Of course, you have me. I'll teach you what you need to know. That is, if you really want to learn.'

I thought about that carefully. It was very generous of him, but I was still on a case. I was a busy cop with a messy career, a runaway wife. I really didn't need another job on top of all that, especially one that seemed so complicated. I had no idea how to be a bookman, what to look for, even with the help of Al Spears.

'I don't know,' I said almost sadly.

'Well, maybe some day, Detective Hollow. I can see you have the collecting bug in you, and you seem to have a real interest in books. I think that some day, we will meet again . . . in books.'

'I hope so, Mr. Spears. Thanks for all your time, I enjoyed it and I think I learned a few things.'

'Well, then our time hasn't been wasted. Good luck, Detective.'

We shook hands and I got ready to leave. I took one last look at the books filling the shelves all around me. They were magical. It was really quite nice to look at them all, and I didn't even notice the cat smell any longer.

On the way out Spears walked me to the door. That's when the attack came. It was fast and furious. I was ambushed by that damn Hemingway. The cat clawed my hand as I fought him off and sent him scampering away. I think he had been going for my gun.

★ ★ ★

The doorbell rang and it was answered right away.

'You? What do you want?'

'Good morning. I have something for you. Something I know you are looking for very much. I have it here in this box.'

'What is it?'

'You'll see. Will you let me in?'

'You're the last person I expected to see.'

'I'm sure, but do you want what I have here, or not?'

'What is it?'

'Are you going to let me in?'

'Very well.'

'Let's go upstairs, into Brian's old office, where we can be alone. Is anyone else in the house?'

'No.'

'The maid, or your pool boy, perhaps?'

'They're all gone, off for the day, and my sister and mother have gone back home. They were getting annoying. We're quite alone.'

'That's good, then lead the way upstairs.'

'All right, follow me. You know, I am surprised to see you. It has been a long time.'

'Yes, it has.'

'Here we are, Brian's old office. Come in.'

'This is the room where Brian was murdered?'

'Yes. He was killed there, right at that very desk.'

'How awful.'

'Yes, it was a surprise, let me tell you.'

'I read it in all the papers. It must have been very difficult for you.'

'Well, we were going to divorce, so . . . '

'Of course.'

'So what do you have for me?'

'It's here in this box. Take it and open it. See for yourself.'

'All right. Let me see. Well . . . it's a book of some kind. Some kind of binder.'

'Not just any old binder.'

'My God! It's Brian's missing Value Book . . . '

'Yes, it is.'

'I've been looking everywhere for this!'

'Well now you have it back.'

'But . . . but that means . . . doesn't that mean you took it? Then that means . . . you're Brian's murderer!'

'*Yes it does.*'

Then two shots were fired, a body fell to the floor, and the visitor quickly left the empty house. It was not yet noon.

★ ★ ★

It was noon and I called Charlie Grant to compare notes.

'I spoke to Spears,' I told my partner over my cell phone. 'He's a good guy. He's pretty upset about McDonald using his name, he was highly insulted and worried about how it will all play out.'

'Huh! Too bad. I still think he's in deeper than he lets on. What about all those names he gave us?'

'Spears told me he knew some of the people, used some of the libraries for research on occasion, like all book people do. I don't think there's much to it though.'

'That's it, Hollow, you don't think,' Grant jibbed.

I let it go, counted to ten, then said, 'So what did you come up with?'

'I visited the two Black women. The ex-maid, Hedger, is a nasty piece of work, she told me McDonald owed her big time for getting her fired. She had a sweet gig, from what she told me. She did nothing at all, just serviced the bookman for pay and perks. Live-in hooker. Nice set-up! Then the wife caught her and McDonald doing the dirty deed in the upstairs bedroom — the same bedroom where hubby and wife slept, not a good idea. Hedger was fired. McDonald ended up dumping her soon after. Our boy had no scruples, no loyalty at all.'

'Yeah, he was one of a kind.'

Grant continued, 'Then I ran by to see the mistress, Alice Larkin. She seems to have moved on from McDonald, wanted nothing to do with him after a brief affair. Seems she dumped him a month or two ago. She wasn't all that interested in him anyway, just his money, and when the money got sparse, so did she. She's an interesting woman.'

'How so?'

'Well, she came on to me,' he said simply.

I was surprised and could imagine the leering smile on Grant's face. I resisted the urge to comment or ask for explicit details.

'Don't you want to hear about it?' he prompted.

'Not really.'

Grant was quiet for a moment, obviously disappointed I had not jumped to the bait to hear about his most recent sexual adventure.

'So what now, Hollow?'

'I guess we finish it up. You revisit the wife, see what she has to say, I'll drop in on the ex-wife again, see what I can come up with there.'

'Zilch, is all,' he said, then hung up.

9

Two Lonely People

Brian McDonald's ex-wife was Sandy Goddard and I remembered her all right from our first visit with her days before. Amazon-big, a figure that didn't quit, very nice looking all ways around. She was still hanging on as a real peach at her age, looking very good, even into her forties. Not bad at all. I didn't mind this part of the job.

Since Beth had left me I'd been lonely and that's no way for any man to go through life. I figured for once I'd got the better assignment here, at least it was the most pleasant, even though Ms. Goddard had admitted to us she was a lesbian. She had no interest in men but at least she seemed to be a pleasant person. Certainly an interesting woman to be around. Not that I was like Grant. I didn't expect anything, other than a decent conversation with her. Which was okay by me. Ms. Goddard seemed to be a far better person than her replacement in McDonald's sordid life — that cold and nasty bitch, Milly. I figured, let Grant talk to Milly all he liked. He was welcome to her and her cold attitude. I got a chill just thinking about that one.

I had called ahead and Ms. Goddard buzzed me up to her apartment. The building and her rooms weren't much to look at, but she sure was. Charlie Grant and I had been here a few days before. Her place was the same sparse environment, not much furniture, just a couch and one recliner surrounding a glass-topped coffee table. No entertainment centre, no TV, but there was a small wet bar against the far wall. I guess she couldn't afford much, just the essentials. Then again, maybe she didn't need or want anything else.

'Detective Hollow,' Ms. Goddard said, and a brief smile came to her face as she let me into her apartment. She was dressed in a tight pair of slacks with a halter top that didn't hide her female assets at all. I gulped nervously, this was going to be a lot more difficult than I had first thought. I realized I'd have to focus on the job at hand, and remember there was no possibility of anything coming of this whatsoever. Well, I'd been married to Beth for years, so I was used to sexual frustration.

'Hello, Ms. Goddard,' I said returning her smile. 'Thanks for seeing me on such short notice.'

'You can call me Sandy,' she said, and there was that mild smile again, as she led me into the living room and over to the couch. 'Drink?'

'No, I'd better not. Not while on duty.'

She laughed rather gaily, and I though, well now, how apropos is that?

'So where's your partner?'

'He's working another part of the case.'

'So he won't be coming here?' she asked. Did I see a glint in her eye?

'No.'

'That's good, because I don't like him. If you don't mind me saying it, he's a real asshole.'

I laughed out loud, rather surprised by my spontaneity but enjoying this bit of mirth at Grant's expense. She joined in with me, with a deep throaty laugh that told me she'd had a lot of practice and enjoyed being joyful. It was nice. It was also the first good laugh I'd had in days, weeks, maybe months.

'You have a nice laugh, Detective, do you know that?' she offered, there was that wan smile again. 'You like to laugh, don't you?'

'Yeah, when I can find something to laugh about.'

'But you don't laugh nearly enough, not like you should. Why is that, Detective Hollow?' she asked me, and I felt something tighten deep within me, tugging at my heart. Was it sadness? Loneliness? Life's realization of all that had been lost?

I looked at her carefully, she looked so nice as she stood there over me with that wan smile, but I began to wonder. What game was she playing? Was she coming on to me? Was she even playing any game at all? I shrugged, probably not. My thoughts went back to what she had said about Grant; that he was an asshole. I smiled, 'You know, you're right about Grant.'

'How could you work with such a moron?'

'Let me tell you, it hasn't been easy, but the brass partnered us together so he and I have no choice. If it's any consolation, Grant dislikes me as much as I dislike him.'

'Oh, I can't believe that, Detective,' then she finished mixing herself a drink and plopped herself down next to me on the couch. She was close, not touching me, but close. I could feel the heat off her body; I could smell the light scent of her perfume. She looked at me and smiled.

'You can call me Sandy,' she said, adding, 'and Detective Hollow sounds so formal. What is your first name?'

'Bentley.'

She laughed, 'Well, that's certainly . . . '

'My friends call me Ben,' I offered quickly.

'Ben, yes, I like that. That's a lot better. Okay, Ben, it's good to see you again.

What can I do for you?'

I switched into full cop mode, all serious, 'Just a few questions.'

'About Brian?' she asked, which seemed odd to me because whatever else would I be there to ask her about?

'Yes, Brian,' I said softly. Was it getting hot in her apartment, or was it just her? Was the air conditioning working right? I looked over at the vent. Yes, it was still blowing cold air into the room. It was late afternoon and a fairly warm day, but it seemed to be getting warmer by the minute.

'Maybe I'll take that drink now,' I said with a smile.

' . . . Sandy?' she prompted.

'Ah, maybe I'll take that drink now, Sandy.'

She smiled back at me rather delight-fully, I thought, which seemed odd. She said, 'Well, that's better.'

Then she stood up and walked over to the bar. When she got up I watched her move, the sway and shape of her body. Female poetry in motion, and she knew it and flaunted it. What a shame she was not only out of my league but not even interested in my gender. Oh well, my bad luck. I watched her joyfully anyway, enjoying the view. I think she knew I was looking at her. It probably got her ego going. I didn't mind, it got me going too.

'What will you have, Ben?'

'Oh, gin and tonic, light on the gin, with ice if you have it, please.'

She fixed the drink and brought it over to me with a sly wink. I sighed, what did that wink mean? Probably nothing. Then she handed me the glass and sat down next to me. Did I miss something or was she sitting closer to me now than she had before?

'I hope you like the drink.'

'I'm sure I will.' I took a sip. 'Yes, that hit's the spot.'

'Good. So what do you want to talk to me about, Ben?'

Every time she talked now she said my name, she smiled at me, then moved closer to me. Nothing overly blatant, you understand, just mild teasing, but she came a little bit closer each time.

We were touching now. I could feel the

heat off her body, drink in the scent of her perfume and I could feel myself becoming aroused. That was not good. I mean, it was good, but it shouldn't be happening. Stuff like that never happens to me. I mean, I was on police business — a damn murder case no less, of which I reminded myself her ex-husband had been the victim. Here I was falling for one of the witnesses — and one I could never have. Oh, she was a fine tease, I'll give her that, but it was all just so damn frustrating.

She moved closer, somehow, and said, 'I like you, Ben, you know that?'

I looked into her eyes and she was smiling at me softly. Her hand suddenly rested on my knee. It did not move. Neither did I.

I looked back at her, a bit surprised. 'Ah, Sandy . . . Ms. Goddard . . . are you . . . are you coming on to me?' Even as I uttered the words I felt like a fool, allowing my fantasies to get the better of me with her teasing. I was immediately sorry that I had let the cat out of the bag about my own feelings towards her. I was acting like a real moron. Like Grant, or worse! I awaited the inevitable reply, some suitably sarcastic and biting retort, probably with the word 'pathetic' in it. I felt suddenly sad, and very lonely. Well, I deserved it. What she said next really did shock me and it had me fumbling for a reply.

'And what if I am, Ben?' she said plainly, her hand still upon my knee, her eyes looking into my own, her mouth slightly open and the red moist lips barely inches from my own.

'But you're . . . a lesbian!' I blurted, like some damn schoolboy.

She just laughed, 'If you must know the truth, I'm not a very good lesbian, Ben. Maybe I'm just a part-timer.'

'Part-timer? What does that mean? Is there such a thing?'

'I sour on men like Brian and move onto women, but then I sour on women and always come back to men when I find one that interests me, I'd like to find a man I can have something meaningful with. Can you be that man, Ben?'

I was in a trance, confused but

delighted. Stuff just happens like that sometimes — but never to me. Whoever would have thought it, certainly not I. Not Bentley Hollow. I bent down to kiss her and her lips met mine.

It had been months since Beth had left me, with no one in between. I had a lot of pent-up feelings to release and it appeared Sandy felt the same way. We released each other wonderfully.

'We've both been ill-treated in love, Ben,' she stated. 'Now is our turn to make up for it.'

I kissed her hard. I guess she was right.

★ ★ ★

An hour or so later we were both pretty well spent. She was lying upon the sheets, dead to the world, but looking very satisfied. I had to smile, I felt pretty good myself.

I was up now, getting out of the bed because of a call coming in on my cell. I'd set the phone to vibrate and thrown it to the floor and forgot all about it while Sandy and I had got down to the business of lovemaking. Now I noticed it was humming at me wildly demanding a response. I shook my head annoyed at the interruption, then quickly picked up my cell phone from the pile of my clothes — I was, after all, still on a case.

I quickly went into the living room so as not to disturb Sandy. She was sleeping dreamily like she didn't have a care in the world. She looked so damn pretty.

'Hollow? Hollow, you there?' The voice at the other end of the phone barked rapidly, impatient.

I sighed, 'Yeah, Grant, what do you want?'

'Been trying to call you for the last hour. You had your phone off?'

'No,' I lied. 'I must be in a dead zone.'

'Yeah, dead zone, my ass. Where the hell are you?'

'The ex-wife's place. So what do you want?' I said trying to hold my patience. I was standing in Sandy's living room talking low so as not to wake her as I talked to my moron partner. I wondered what Grant wanted now.

'Listen, Hollow, I went to see the wife

like we planned. She's dead. I found her shot twice. Looks like it was done early this morning. The crime scene guys and the Captain are on their way over. You'd better make a beeline here, pronto!' Grant ordered.

Milly McDonald dead? Murdered? I shook my head to clear it, trying to think this through.

'Okay, Grant, thanks for the heads-up,' I said grateful to my idiot partner as I tried to absorb the shock of this new development in the case and what it might mean.

I shook my head and shut the phone. I had to get dressed and out of there fast, but I didn't want to wake Sandy. Not just yet. I remember how she looked in bed, so peaceful in her lust-induced slumber.

I walked out of the living room and down the hall to go back into her bedroom to get my clothes and get dressed. On the way I had to take a leak so I looked for the bathroom. I opened the first closed door off that hallway, but it wasn't the bathroom just another bedroom — a room I'd never been in before. Then I froze. The room was surrounded by wooden shelves on all four walls and upon those shelves were books. A lot of books. Books everywhere!

I was stunned. I looked inside amazed and then walked around the room looking at all the volumes of what looked like expensive first editions. It was a relatively small grouping of books, but it looked like primo stuff. Some pretty old and nice condition editions, I assumed all were first editions.

I was intrigued, but initially, that was all I felt. After all, Sandy had been married to a major book dealer for years, she was also an intelligent, educated woman, so it was quite natural, maybe even essential, that she would have books in her place. Maybe even a lot of books.

Then I saw it!

The thick binder laying on the middle of the desktop all by itself. I could hardly have missed it. It was the same description as Brian McDonald's missing Value Book. I walked over slowly, nervously, well aware of just what it might mean if this was in fact McDonald's

151

missing book. Could it be?

Nah, I told myself. No, it had to be a coincidence. Maybe Sandy had her own record book, maybe she'd even taken the idea from her former husband? Hadn't Spears told me all serious dealers and collectors had such a book or kept such records? That made sense. That had to be it, I thought. That would be normal, not a coincidence — but a little voice inside me told me it was otherwise. What it told me I just didn't want to believe.

Even as I opened the binder and read what was written there I knew the truth of it all now.

I was startled by the voice that came from behind me.

'So you found it, Ben,' Sandy said bluntly, and I turned to see her standing there totally nude, framed in the doorway, a gun in her hand levelled right at me.

I sighed, deflated with disappointment more than fear, not knowing how to react, so I asked the obvious question, 'You killed Brian?'

'Yes, I did, Ben, and I also shot that bitch Milly. The world's a better place without her. I should get a medal for that one, let me tell you. You'll hear about Milly soon. I'm sure it will make the news.'

'Grant just called me about it, he found her body an hour ago,' I told her, hardly noticing her nudity now, or my own. It was an almost ludicrous scene, us standing there naked in a room full of rare books. The gun in her hand levelled at me was the only sobering equation in that crazy scene.

'So what now?' I asked, my eyes locking on that damn gun she had pointed at me.

'I don't know, Ben,' she said plainly. I could see genuine sadness in her features, maybe even a tear of regret streaming down her cheek. 'Why the hell did you have to snoop around? Why the hell did you come in here? I had the door closed, you shouldn't have opened it.'

'I was looking for the bathroom,' I said lamely.

She laughed lightly, smiled delightfully at that. 'Men!'

I said, 'Sandy, are you going to kill me too? You know you won't get away with this now.'

153

'I know that, Ben.'

'Why don't you give me the gun?'

She pointed it at me hard, then fire came into her eyes, 'No. I have to think about this. I have to think . . . '

I tried another tack. 'Why did you do it? Why did you kill Brian, and why did you write that message on his desk, 'Book Collectors, Go To Hell!'?'

She moved the gun so it centred on my heart, not a good sign.

'He not only cheated on me with other women, which was bad enough, I could handle that. What I couldn't handle was that he cheated me out of my father's books in the divorce settlement.'

'You father's books?' I blurted, not understanding what she was telling me and showing it in my face.

She smiled indulgently, explained, 'When we were married I brought my father's books to the marriage which were combined with Brian's. My father had a very valuable collection and I inherited them upon his death.'

'But you told Grant and me you didn't collect anything, especially books!'

She smiled sweetly, 'I lied, Ben. A woman's prerogative. I didn't have to tell you and that other detective my personal business.'

'So Brian screwed you in the divorce settlement?'

'Yes and no. He wanted all the books so he gave me the house and some cash. At the time it seemed like a good deal — all I was giving up was my father's musty old books. Who cared about them? Certainly not I, at the time,' she admitted sadly. 'Then I found out just how much they were worth. Brian built his business on the books he stole from me. My father's books. I know I gave them up, I know I should have been more knowledgeable about their value — but he was my husband, Ben. I trusted him. When he told me they were not worth all that much I believed him. They were just dad's old books, to me. At that time I never took an interest in books or the book business.'

'I see.'

'I trusted Brian. He should have let me know their true value and given me a fair price for them, instead he had all that information locked away in his damn secret Value Book. Then during the divorce he gave me a settlement that looked generous, as long as he kept all the books. The books were all that he ever really wanted. It wasn't fair. I wanted them back.'

'So he not only stole from you. I heard he stole from everyone. You know that he stole from some university libraries and their special collections also?'

'The bastard!'

'Then why do Milly McDonald?' I asked carefully. We were standing there naked, but any sexual interest had long since diminished and been lost. The gun she held pointed at me I now realized was probably the very weapon she had used to murder McDonald's wife bare hours earlier that morning.

'That greedy bitch! If I wasn't going to allow Brian to get away with keeping all my father's — now my — rare and valuable books, there was no way in hell I was going to let Milly get them all. I knew about the divorce, so I knew I had to act fast before the books were split up. That would make things too difficult. I had to act while they were all in one place. Milly was not a good and trusting soul like me, Ben. She would have made sure she got half the books, probably the better half, if I knew her like I thought I did. I had no choice but to act before that happened.'

'Give me the gun, Sandy,' I said firmly.

She just laughed, 'You look so funny there, Ben.'

I essayed a wan grin.

'Ben. I'm so sorry.' Then she added softly, 'I guess I made a mess out of everything.'

All I saw now were her hard eyes looking at me and the barrel of that gun pointed straight at my heart.

'You don't want to do this, Sandy,' I pleaded, trying to hide the fear I felt and the desperation in my voice. 'You don't want to kill me. You'll never get away with it.'

'I know that,' she replied softly, like she was already in a far away place and it was our last goodbye. She gave me a sad little smile, 'I'll miss you, Ben, I really will. I just want you to know that. But what I wrote is true, book collectors do go to hell, sometimes.'

She looked at me firmly, eye to eye. I could see the determination in her now. It was scary. I knew she had made a hard decision to cut her losses and that it was coming to fruition very soon.

I shuddered, tightly closed my eyes and waited. Then I heard the shot. The single report seemed to last a lifetime and it reverberated throughout the small room, echoing off all the shelves filled so tightly with so many books.

I stood there frozen, in panic and astonishment. Then I opened my eyes and saw Sandy's lush body fall to the floor with a hard thump, the pistol dropping from her limp fingers. Blood spurted from a wound in her temple.

'Sandy!' I shouted. 'Sandy! No!'

She looked at me strangely as I ran over to her and cradled her head in my arms, the blood madly gushing like a stream over our bodies. Her eyes looked blank, dull, I knew she was slipping away. Then she suddenly focused on me for an instant and a brief smile came to her lips,

'Ben ... I do like you ... ' she whispered, 'and I guess you do care.'

'Yes, I do,' I spoke softly, between my tears. 'Sandy? Sandy!'

I cried as she died there in my arms. I lay there with her for hours, the two of us wrapped together with her blood all over our bodies. I hardly noticed it. I couldn't move, I didn't know what to do. My police training wanted to kick in — I know what I should have done — but I just couldn't do it.

I cried a lot that night and I let myself sleep in her dead arms.

★　★　★

They found us early the next morning. They came for me when I never showed at the McDonald house. Charlie Grant was the first one to come into the room and see us, then Captain Wallace and the crime scene team.

I vaguely remember seeing Grant looking down at us with shock, then an evil twisted leer came to his face when he saw our nakedness.

The crime scene team took their photos, then one of them helped me up from Sandy's body. Then they took more photos of her alone. One of the guys dropped a towel over me and then sat me in a chair.

I looked at Charlie Grant with rage and unabashed hatred. This partnership was about to end — right now — the hard way.

Charlie Grant came over to me, a sly, wicked grin on his face.

'So tell me, what was she like?'

I stood up from my chair and suddenly hit Grant with a brick-hard fist straight into his face. It was a pile-driver blow that must have broken his nose — blood was spurting everywhere from his face — he rolled over and cried like a baby.

'This partnership is over!' I shouted, closing the subject forever.

I looked at Captain Wallace, he'd witnessed the entire scene, as well as all the crime scene techs. I was right in it now. I realized this had not been such a good career move but it felt so damn good I didn't care just then.

'You'll find Brian McDonald's missing

Value Book on her desk there. It proves Sandy Goddard was the killer of Brian McDonald, her gun will match the bullets that killed Milly McDonald also.'

Then I calmly walked out of the room and down the hall into Sandy's bedroom. I gathered my clothes. I ignored the blood on me. It was Sandy's blood. It was the only thing I had left from her now. As I got dressed Captain Wallace came into the bedroom.

He looked at me for a long moment in utter shock. I looked back hard, daring him to speak. Finally he did.

'This is a real mess, Hollow,' he told me, not without some sympathy, but I could see he had a job to do and no nonsense could be allowed now. 'You found the killer and closed the case, which is good. You did a good job, but your methods are damn irregular . . .'

'You mean sleeping with a witness?'

'Sleeping with the murderer, Hollow,' he corrected me with a sharp stare.

I thought it was a minor point to remind Wallace that at the time we had begun to make love Sandy had only been a witness, so I said nothing. I'd never thought of her as a suspect and certainly not a murderer.

Wallace looked at me grimly, shook his head sadly and continued, 'When this gets out, and it will, Hollow, it will cause all kinds of unpleasantness in the media for me, and for the department. I think it might be best . . . '

'Don't worry yourself about it, Captain,' I said as I put on my pants and tucked in my shirt. 'I've got the time, I'm putting in my papers. I'll be gone by the end of the week.'

'That might be best, Hollow' he said with a deep sigh of relief, and just a hint of regret.

'I know it will be,' I replied and walked out of the bedroom, leaving him standing there alone. On the way out I shouted back to him, 'You need me for anything, you know how to reach me. You'll have a written statement from me in a couple of days. Now I'm going home — I've had enough. Enough of Charlie Grant, enough of you, enough of this damn department and enough of being a cop.'

Part 2

The Fenton Art Class Murder

Bentley Hollow looked at the various pieces of collectable glass in the four breakfronts in his home with a bit of awe and not a little consternation. He had quite a nice collection of Depression glassware, but he still kept buying more when he could find it. Hollow and his wife had always had a passion collecting, but the glass was the only legacy remaining from his marriage to Beth. When Beth left him — she got a doctor and his mansion — Bentley just got the glass. Most of it, at any rate, but Beth had taken some of the better, valuable pieces. That was so like Beth.

All in all, Hollow realized now, he had made out best in the deal. Beth had divorced her doctor lover after less than a year and after receiving the less than hefty settlement she wanted, had made overtures that she might want to come back to Bentley. It all hurt so much. Hollow got tough and blew her off; he'd had enough of her games and all the turmoil she'd caused. She'd wrecked his life and he was just getting back on track.

Hollow had recently retired from the city police, it had been a rough end to a long career. Now he was just trying to enjoy his collecting and antiquing adventures, going to shows, flea markets and yard sales. He said he wanted to deal in antiques as a business but he always seemed to buy more than he sold! Now he was also interested in old books, a love embedded in him by Al Spears, an old bookseller he'd met on the Brian McDonald murder case. That had been a rough one; he still thought of Sandy Goddard and her suicide. Now he just wanted calm and peace, but he also needed to make some money, so he took a case from time to time. He had rather simple needs these days, and with his pension, was able to make ends meet and even support his collecting habit. Every once and a while, if things were getting tight he took on cases — PI work paid better than the city. So when the daughter of an elderly dealer called for help, the case seemed to kill two birds with one stone.

Her mom Dorothy Glidden, owner of the West Shore Antiques Mart, she told him, had been found dead in her store. The cops deemed it to be death from natural causes. Dorothy was an elderly grandmother with a history of heart problems. The cops found that the register, never overflowing with filthy lucre in the best of times, held just $88 in cash and coin. It had not been touched. Neither had any of her store stock been found missing, all was orderly in the store and on the shelves, so the cops said there had not been any robbery.

That's when Dorothy's daughter, Carol, called Bentley Hollow and asked for his help. Since he was an ex-cop and also knowledgeable in the antique and collectibles area, Hollow was considered by Carol to be the natural person to investigate what happened to her mom.

Carol had taken over her mother's business and felt there was more to the story than the cops and coroner had made out.

After Hollow spoke to the daughter he wasn't so sure she was correct in her suspicions but he decided to look into it. In the course of his own collecting interests he had been in Dorothy's store on a few occasions and purchased the odd item from her. Hollow had liked the little old lady, and he liked her store. It was quaint and not overpriced, but that was because her stock was strictly lower level merchandise. Most all of her items were minor to moderate in quality, the more common pieces such as cups, saucers, smaller plates. She also had a few small bowls, but none of the higher price pieces, like grill plates, pitchers, batter jugs, or decorative items such as art deco lamps with coloured glass shades. Many of Dorothy's items were also chipped, so collectors had to buy with care from her even though the prices reflected the condition.

Dorothy had very little Jadeite, which had become so popular over the last few years. Hollow collected this with a passion. In fact, he was actually quite happy when Martha Stewart got sent away. Not for her stock crimes though, but because the home diva had cornered the market on Jadeite and he felt she was responsible for driving up prices. She'd even added insult to injury by having the glassware reissued by her company at collectible prices. Hollow knew he could never touch the prices asked for many of the rare quality pieces these days, and he lamented the low prices he used to pay for items in the good old days before Martha. How many pieces he'd passed up; had he only known back then, he would have bought up all of it — and retired from the force years earlier!

Dorothy's store also sold pottery. She had mostly later items of lower quality, but there was the occasional small McCoy or Roseville piece, usually with a tiny nick here or there that significantly brought down the value, but also the price. She had hardly anything worth over a hundred dollars and nothing with a price tag much higher than that. In fact, she had nothing on the big money level, and certainly nothing worth killing for. That is, until Hollow spoke with Dorothy's daughter, Carol. She told him about a Fenton pitcher and reamer set, #1619 in Pekin Blue glass, from 1933 — which she said was worth at least five thousand dollars!

Hollow fondly remembered the clear glass reamer his mother had used to squeeze his orange juice for breakfast. That was in the 1950s when he had been a child. He would watch her as she halved an orange, then pressed the cut edge into the reamer, turning it back and forth, so the juice ran down to collect at the bottom. The Pekin Blue reamer was like that, but it sat atop a pitcher, so the juice flowed right into it, all ready to pour. It was a nice item.

Hollow found out that this piece had been Dorothy's pride and joy and the only valuable and rare piece she owned. It wasn't until after the funeral and Carol was going through some things in the store, she'd even noticed it was missing. The piece hadn't been for sale, it had not been displayed publicly in the store. For fun, she said her mom put a price of one million dollars on it, written on a store tag at the bottom. She always said that's what someone would have to offer her to part with it. Hollow realized whoever took the piece knew that Dorothy had it, and knew that it was valuable. It was a family piece, understood by all that it was to be handed down by mom, to daughter, when Dorothy passed away. Only Carol never expected that to be so soon, and she was heartbroken when she told Hollow about it.

Hollow couldn't believe a reamer set could be worth that much — until Carol showed him the Fenton Glass price guides. There it was five thousand dollars, and the guide was more than five years old! How'd he miss that? Hollow knew this put a different spin on things, that there had been a thief, and probably a killer as well. It had to be one of Dorothy's confidants or collector friends, someone she was close to. She had no employees. So knowing all this he went right to the cops.

★ ★ ★

Hollow was surprised that the police offered him no help. Detective Paul Ryan had been a case-closer when Bentley Hollow had worked with him a few years back before he'd retired from the job. That had been during the bookman murders when he'd been partnered up with Charlie Grant, which had ended in the suicide of the lovely, luscious Sandy Goddard. Hollow tried not to think about it, or her . . . Ryan reminded him of his partner on that case, Charlie Grant, though he was not as bad. Ryan's attitude was that the old lady had died of natural causes, and since it was backed up by the coroner — that was that! Nothing had been disturbed in the store, so there was no crime. Ryan got to add one more check on his case-closed list and got a pat on the head and a cookie from the Captain. Captain Wallace, still hanging on after so many years, liked that Ryan showed results, he didn't much care whether the results were right or wrong Hollow suspected, he just wanted results so things would go away. Ryan had made Dorothy Glidden's murder go away and

Bentley Hollow didn't like that one bit.

'So what happened to this Fenton Art Glass piece?' Hollow asked Ryan, figuring he had just broken open the case. He smiled to himself; it was just like the old days.

'One piece! Come on Ben, she probably sold it, or broke it,' Ryan offered without any interest at all, and Hollow realized that it *was* just like the old days.

'Paul, it's supposed to be worth *five thousand dollars!*' Hollow was adamant now.

'Nah, no way, not for a piece of old glass! Maybe if it were Tiffany or something . . . Come on, even you said she had no top quality merch there.'

'Yeah, right, but this one piece . . . '

'Forget it, Ben, nice try,' Ryan offered with a shrug. 'Look, I know what it's gotta be like, being retired and all, got nothing to do all day, figure you get back in the action, eh? Well, go home, Ben, sit in the sun, enjoy your senior years.'

'Screw you, Paul!' Hollow growled, Ryan's words hurt more than he wanted to admit.

Paul Ryan just laughed, walked away.

'You're not going to build a case-closed percentage on this old lady's death!' Hollow barked at Ryan as he walked out of the room. 'She was murdered and it was during a robbery!'

Ryan stopped, turned, he wasn't laughing any more, 'Murdered? No way! The old lady died of a heart attack, pure and simple.'

'Yeah? Well, it was a heart attack brought on by a robbery!' Hollow insisted.

'Prove it, Hollow!' Ryan barked, angry at having his precious motives questioned so publicly in the squad room like that. 'Murdered for a juice glass! Get the hell out of here! The case is closed!'

'Your mind is closed!' Hollow barked back but he left the room.

Ryan laughed, muttered something that sounded like 'asshole', and walked away.

Hollow left the precinct, knowing he had cut another tie to his past career and could expect no help from his brother cops now.

* ★ ★

Bentley Hollow liked glass and he looked through his guides partly for research, but mostly for pleasure. He loved the vivid colours and wonderful patterns. He liked early American Sandwich Glass, anything hand blown, old pottery, even cookie jars. There was so much to choose from. Each piece had it's own beauty and grace, but his favourite was Depression Era Glass.

Other people liked another popular collectible style called Carnival Glass, also made by Fenton, from 1907 to 1939. This was extremely colourful, with bright and often iridescent colours. Most Carnival Glass pieces had been giveaways to customers at gas stations or movie theatres in the 1930s, who were given a piece after each purchase, or bought for pennies at department stores like F.W. Woolworth's.

Fenton also made what it called 'Art Glass' and this is what Hollow was concentrating on now. These pieces were made in different patterns such as vases, lamps, console bows, pitchers, candlesticks and other items for more everyday use. Such as juice reamers. He didn't collect Fenton so he had to research it. When he did he was surprised at the value placed on the Fenton coloured reamers. They were all very collectible.

However, Hollow's research told him that the Pekin Blue Pitcher and reamer set was the most expensive piece of Fenton Art Glass there was. Officially, it was from 1933, #1619, Fenton Art Glass Pitcher and Reamer set in the Pekin Blue glass pattern. Blue was the rarest colour, though you'd never know that by looking at it, and could not know that without a price guide. It was hard for him to believe the prices of these reamers — he had a lot of glassware, after Beth's leaving his most expensive piece was a few hundred dollars — but that seemed like peanuts now! This was important because he discovered there were identical pieces in the same pattern but in different coloured glass, and at often-lower prices. These included Green Transparent, Chinese Yellow, and Black glass. There were also reproductions galore — which you had to be aware of. Hollow could see where this could get confusing real fast but he studied the relevant books and photos, and made a few phone calls for clarification. Soon he was on his way. He was sure he was looking for someone who had known the value of this particular piece.

Dorothy Glidden's store was full of old glass, much of it from the Depression Era that runs from the 1920s until the 1950s as far as collectors are concerned, but he had never seen anything in the multi-thousand dollar price range like that Fenton pitcher and reamer set. Hollow never would have guessed Dorothy had such an expensive piece in her store, and at first he had some suspicion that perhaps Carol was making a false insurance claim. He'd have to check that and see if she claimed anything. He also wondered if she had any paper on the piece, photos perhaps, and knew he'd have to check that too. In the meantime, if a rare and valuable pitcher and reamer set had been stolen from Dorothy it would mean there was a killer. He'd have to find that killer, and once he found him, he was sure he had the motive already. Or so he hoped. Then when he went to the cops again that blockhead Ryan and his boss would have to listen to him.

★ ★ ★

The next day Hollow began an exhaustive search by phone and over the Internet for any collector or dealer who had a #1619 Fenton pitcher and reamer set in Pekin Blue for sale.

It was long and exhausting work. Even the specialists in Fenton Art Glass didn't have such a rare piece in that distinctive blue glass pattern. One collector had the same item in Green Transparent for sale. A dealer said he knew where he could get his hands on a similar piece in Chinese Yellow, but as for the rare Pekin Blue, 'I've only seen one in 20 years and you'd have to kill the woman to get it from her!'

Hollow thanked them both but said that he was really interested in the Pekin Blue only and that he was the buyer for a wealthy collector for whom money was no object. Nothing got a dealer's juices flowing more than those last four words

— 'money was no object.'

Hollow called every antique and collectibles store in town, and quite a few out of town. He made calls to shops in New York and Los Angeles. He spent countless hours on the Internet and searched eBay and other collectibles auction sites. He called auction houses and big name collectors. He was amazed at how friendly and helpful everyone was.

On the fourth day he'd exhausted all the stores and the Internet. It seemed no one had a set, not an original one anyway, or knew of one — whether it was for sale or not. His story, about being the buyer for a wealthy private collector who just had to have this particular Fenton piece hadn't gotten a bite. He also mentioned that a considerable finder's fee would go to anyone who could help him obtain this item. The sharks were out there but so far the right piece remained elusive.

Hollow knew collectors, but he knew dealers even better — the buzz was out there now about the Pekin Blue and the big cash payday for anyone who had it. He just wondered if a person who had killed for this piece would part with it. It didn't seem likely. Hollow knew how things often went down in this game — the piece would just disappear and eventually fill a spot in some wealthy person's collection. Now Hollow just waited and hoped that someone would contact him.

He didn't have long to wait before he received a flurry of phone calls and a dozen emails — none of which panned out. Most could be discounted immediately, or with just one probing question. Then he got a call the next afternoon that piqued his interest.

'Is this Bentley Hollow?' a faraway voice came over the phone. Hollow said that it was.

'Then you're the guy who's looking for some Fenton glass, aren't you?' the man said.

'Specifically, a Fenton pitcher and reamer set, item #1619 from 1933 in Pekin Blue glass, yes, I am looking for such a piece,' Hollow replied hopefully, but trying to keep calm and not scare the caller off.

'Yeah, that's what I mean.'

'So you have it?' Hollow asked, then quickly added, 'My client can pay whatever you ask . . . '

There was silence at the other end of the phone and Hollow felt he could imagine the man — and perhaps the very killer of Dorothy Glidden? — licking his lips in greed and anticipation at the prospect of being paid 'whatever he asked.'

'Yeah, I know where I can get it,' the voice was anxious now and Hollow was immediately suspicious.

'What do you mean 'get it'? I don't want you to steal the piece, this has to be on the up and up,' Hollow offered, just to see what the guy's comeback would be.

The voice at the other end of the phone had suddenly become silent.

Bentley Hollow thought that over. He had to be careful here, this could just be a scam — some con artist who had heard the buzz he'd put out to the collector community about the Fenton and the cash he'd pay. It could just be someone who figured to get him alone and rob him. On the other hand, this could be the real thing — hopefully this man had the glass and needed money right away. But this was his 50th phone call, all 49 priors had been dead ends, so Hollow figured it was probably a scam as well and was about to brush off the guy. After all he realized, this guy didn't really sound like anyone who was in the antique field — more like some low-level under-educated crook looking for an opportunity to use information he'd come across in his travels to scam a pile of cash.

However, something kept nagging at Hollow's mind. If he had the Fenton, how did this fellow know to rob that one very valuable piece — out of everything else in Dorothy's store? Hollow realized he'd have to be more circumspect in his inquiries. Then the man suddenly blurted out a question showing his impatience and nervousness.

'What did you say?' Hollow responded, he wanted the man to repeat his words so he had time to better gauge him.

'Look, man, you want the glass or not?' the voice said hastily. 'I can't wait all day, my brother has the glass — see he's the one that collects it — but if the price is right he could be convinced to sell. So what's your price?'

Hollow thought quickly. Perhaps this wasn't a scam after all? If this man's brother collected the glassware, that explained a lot. He made up a figure, which he thought would appeal to the man's greed, but not too high, so as to reveal whether or not the man knew what he had — but first he asked him his name.

There was silence for a moment, then the man said, 'Mr. Jones.'

Hollow didn't believe him for a second but he wasn't going to worry about identifying the man now. 'Well, Mr. Jones, I represent a wealthy private collector, who . . . '

'Yeah, I know all about that,' Jones interrupted impatiently. 'What I want to know is what you'll pay for the blue glass?'

Bentley Hollow nodded, said, 'I can pay you a hundred dollars.'

Jones just laughed, 'Come on, man, get serious!'

Hollow was purposely bidding low to see if the guy knew the value. Then he decided to double his offer, 'All right, two hundred . . . '

'You're wasting my time . . . ' Jones said angry now, anxious, even bitter.

Hollow made an audible sigh of resignation, 'All right then, how much do you want for it?'

'A piece like this one, it should get me at least five thousand!' Jones said bluntly.

Hollow thought over what he had learned.

Jones was quiet for a long moment, no doubt mentally counting his money.

Hollow wondered now if the man even had a brother. He had to figure out how Jones had known Dorothy had this glass set, and how he had known to take that particular piece — and no other — out of all the hundreds of such coloured glass pieces in her shop? He obviously knew the value — but how?

Hollow realized he had to set up a meet with Jones and then find out just who he really was. Maybe follow him? But first he had to make sure that this particular

Fenton piece was not only the correct item but that it was the *actual* item stolen from Dorothy Glidden's store.

'Fine, Mr. Jones. I agree. Five thousand dollars. Now how can we meet to complete the transaction?'

'Okay, now you're talking! Bring the money with you. It has to be all cash, nothing larger than twenties. I don't like big bills. Meet me at The Blue Note, it's a bar over on Ninth Street. You know it?'

'Yes, I know where it is.'

'I'll be seated alone at a booth in the back.'

'Just make sure it's not a repro,' Hollow said.

'Don't worry, it's real, just make sure you bring the cash,' Jones replied anxiously.

Once he hung up the phone, Bentley Hollow felt dirty and nervous. Was he going alone to meet a man who would rob him? Or, even worse, a deadly killer? Hollow quickly made another phone call, this time to his last friend on the police force — he filled her in on his plan and just hoped that she really was still a friend.

The Blue Note was a bar with a restaurant in the back, located in a neighbourhood that had seen better days. The place wasn't particularly crowded up front but there were some people who were obviously regulars watching baseball on TV. Hollow walked toward the bar and asked the man there to make him a rum and coke. He needed it. He was going to meet a man who could possibly be a thief and a murderer. He had no gun, and only the word of a friend who had told him if he needed help, it would be there. Hollow didn't have many friends these days, he'd thought Paul Ryan had been a friend but he had been wrong about him. He wondered what else he was wrong about? Now he was nervous, but he knew this is what he had to do if he wanted to solve this case and catch the killer.

Turning from the bar his eyes scanned the place. It was dark and full of shadows, and there were booths in the back just like Jones had said, five or six of them. They were mostly filled with underage kids from the neighbourhood who shouldn't have been in the bar in the first place. There was also a couple sitting close together like lovers. Hollow envied them, it just reminded him how alone he had become since Beth had left him. Then Hollow's eyes looked onto the form of a man sitting by himself in the next booth, over in the corner.

The booth was shadowed and dark, but Hollow could see the shopping bag upon the table nearest the wall.

Hollow left his drink on the bar and walked back toward the booth with the lone man in it.

'Mr. Jones?'

'Yeah, sit down. You got the cash?'

Hollow didn't reply to that question, instead he said, 'You have the glass?'

Jones nodded to the bag on the table.

'Well?' Hollow said. 'Let me see it.'

'Let me see the five thou.'

'No way, I have to see the glass first.'

Jones' face grew hard and dark but he finally motioned to the bag with his thumb, 'Take a look.'

Hollow did just that. He opened the

bag and saw the pitcher with the reamer on top of it and carefully took it out and examined it closely. It only took him a minute to notice the store sticker on the bottom of each piece that said 'West Shore Antique Mart', which was the name of Dorothy Glidden's store. This one said the price was $1,000,000 in red ink. Hollow smiled, it was Dorothy's all right. Now Hollow knew he had his thief — and maybe the murderer as well — but who was he?

'Well?' Jones prompted, nervous, impatient.

The man was jumpy, which might have been nothing more than criminal fear, or it could have meant something else. Hollow put that thought away for the moment as he asked Jones, as innocently as he could say it, 'Where did you get this?'

'That ain't no business of yours,' Jones answered defensively, then gruffly added, 'Did you bring the cash?'

'Yes, I brought the cash,' Hollow said as he stood up, making it look like he was reaching in his pocket to withdraw a wad of bills to pay Jones with. Instead he blurted out, 'Okay, it's good. The glass is from the store, it has the markings on it.'

Jones shot a look to Hollow, 'Who you talking to? What the hell . . .'

Jones jumped up ready to run but just then the big hand of Detective Ed Stanhope pulled him back and turned him around, while Detective Jackie Harris pulled back Jones' arms and locked hand cuffs tightly on his wrists. It was the couple from the next booth.

'What the hell is this!' Jones barked as Stanhope pulled him off to the side.

Bentley Hollow showed the Fenton pitcher and reamer set to Harris. 'This is it.'

'Pretty stuff,' she said, looking it over carefully and noting the store sticker on the bottom of the glass that Hollow pointed out to her. 'I can see why people collect it.'

'This piece was stolen from the old woman's store. I believe she was so terrorized by the theft that she had a heart attack and died on the spot,' Hollow told Harris and Stanhope. 'At least that's what I thought at first. Once I met 'Mr. Jones' here, another thought occurred to me.'

'What's that?' Harris asked.

'Drop dead!' Jones barked.

'Shut your face!' Stanhope said, pulling Jones away from the table by the cuffs.

Hollow continued, 'You see, I kept trying to figure out how this all happened. Dorothy Glidden only had this one valuable piece in her shop and it wasn't for sale, nor was it on display to the public. Only a very close collector or friend would even have known about this item at all. Or a family member.'

Detective Jackie Harris nodded. 'Makes sense.'

'I think if you look in 'Mr. Jones'' wallet, you'll find that his name isn't Jones at all.' Hollow said allowing some triumph in his voice.

Detective Harris did just that. She frisked Jones, quickly pulling out his wallet, bringing out his driver's licence, 'Yeah, his name is Jonathan Glidden.'

'I'd bet this is Dorothy Glidden's grandson.' Hollow looked at the young man with disgust, 'Did you kill her because she might turn you in?'

Glidden looked up sadly, 'I didn't want her to know it was me. I had on a ski mask, but she pulled it off. She didn't say anything when she saw it was me, just stood there all bug-eyed and then she just keeled over. I didn't kill her . . . '

Hollow nodded, it made sense with what he knew the facts to be. 'I think that's really what caused the old girl to have the heart attack. Not so much that her priceless Fenton pitcher and reamer set was being stolen right before her eyes — but that it was by her own *grandson*. I also have a hunch that if you roll up his shirtsleeves you'll find track marks show-ing heroin addiction. He was going to sell the glassware to get money to go on the mother of all drug binges.'

'Come on you, let's go!' Detective Stanhope barked, and he took out Jonathan Glidden.

'I'm glad you guys could make it on such short notice,' Hollow said to Harris.

Detective Jackie Harris smiled, and Bentley Hollow was reminded all over again why he'd fallen for her in the first place a year ago. He was sorry it hadn't worked out, but they had somehow remained friends.

'You know Ryan and Captain Wallace won't like this, you getting involved and all, but they'll get used to it,' Harris said with a wink. 'I can't wait to write the report: I take a closed case all neatly wrapped up with death by natural causes — reopen it as a murder case. Then, since we have the perp, we solve the murder and close the case again! They won't like that one bit. But since we have the killer, they'll have to accept it. Just don't expect Ryan and Wallace to admit they were wrong on this.'

'Thanks, Jackie,' Hollow said, picking up the Pekin Blue reamer set.

Detective Harris had to pry the reamer out of Hollow's hands, 'And this is evidence.' She gave him a half smile, 'You take care, Bentley Hollow.'

* * *

West Shore Antique Mart reopened two weeks later as Dorothy's Antique Mart.

Dorothy Glidden's daughter, Carol, had taken over ownership of the store and renamed it in honour of her mother.

'It's terrible about my nephew, Mr. Hollow,' Carol Glidden said. She was arranging things in the store when he had come by for his cheque. 'We all knew Jonathan had problems with drugs but we never thought he would do something like steal from my mom, from his own grandmother. He's my brother, Charles's oldest son. I don't think he meant — you know, for mom to die.'

'I don't think so,' Hollow replied softly.

'What will happen to him now?' she asked, trying to hold back her concern.

Hollow shrugged, 'Difficult to say, it's up to the court to decide. He committed a robbery, and in the commission of that crime a woman died. It's not first degree murder, but he could get some prison time, and he needs detox.'

'Well, the detox could only help him,' Carol Glidden agreed.

Bentley Hollow nodded, his eyes drawn to the stunning blue glass of the Fenton pitcher and reamer set the police had just returned. Carol now placed it in a prominent display case behind the counter. 'That Pekin Blue sure looks lovely there.'

'Yes, it really is quite beautiful,' Carol Glidden said. 'It looks so nice here in the store where people can see it and enjoy it now.'

'But not for sale?' Hollow asked with a smile, sure he already knew the answer.

'No, it's not for sale, Mr. Hollow. It was mom's prize possession and it will always remind me of her. She always said she wanted me to have it after she died.'

Bentley Hollow smiled, saying his goodbye to Carol Glidden and wishing her well. He hadn't been paid that much for his service but he figured it might just do as a down payment on a Fenton pitcher and reamer set in Chinese Yellow glass a dealer had called him about a few days ago. He hoped it was still available. After all, Bentley Hollow was also a collector ... *and now he was also collecting Fenton!*

Part 3

The Bruba Rombic Robbery

'Mr. Hollow,' the voice over the telephone pleaded. 'My name is John Castle and I'm calling because my wife and I are very worried about our Ruba Rombic.'

'Ruba . . . who?'

'Rombic! Ruba Rombic!' the man at the other end of the line said intently. 'It's not a 'who', it's a 'what'. Ever hear of it?'

'Okay, Ruba . . . What?' I replied, confusion and annoyance creeping into my voice as I wondered just what this fellow wanted. Since my wife had left me and I'd retired from the police, I'd led a rather quiet life these days, buying and selling antique collectable glassware, playing a little golf, buying some old books.

'Ruba Rombic, it's Depression Glass,' he explained.

'Oh,' I replied with a shrug. Though I collected Depression Glass, I'd never heard of it.

'Mr. Hollow, I read about you in the

local paper last year, that thing about the Fenton Art Glass and the old lady who died.'

'Yes,' I replied carefully.

'So I thought I'd call to hire you. Our Ruba Rombic has been stolen and my wife and I are at our wits end. We want you to get it back for us.'

'Ah, look, Mr . . . ?'

'Castle, John Castle. My wife's name is Susan.'

'Well, Mr. Castle, I'm retired now. I don't even know what this Ruba Rombic is and even if I did, I'm not a licensed private investigator. You need to go to the police if you have been the victim of a robbery.'

'I know that, but you're a collector,' Castle said seriously. 'That's what matters most.'

So that's how I got into it. The next day I drove out to Woodmere and the nice big house that John and Susan Castle lived in. The Castles' castle.

He was a retired industrialist and she did volunteer work and collected antiques. They seemed like nice people. They were

198

both big art deco collectors, which was a bit out of my area of interest and affordability. I collected Depression Era glassware — but I soon discovered the two areas did overlap — they overlapped especially when it came to Ruba Rombic.

I shook my head as I looked at the photos Mrs. Castle showed me of the precious glassware items she said had been stolen from their home.

'Aren't they lovely!' she gushed.

Could she be serious? I kept mum. It certainly appeared to be some kind of glassware, Depression Era for sure but I'd never seen the likes before. I'll give them this, the stuff was certainly unique — there was nothing quite like it in Depression glass. I learned later that it was made from 1928 to 1932 by the Consolidated Lamp and Glass Company — designed by Ruben Haley — but the main thing about it to me was that it was so damn incredibly ugly. I mean, it looked like something created by a mad man's warped brain, or a bad Flintstones episode. It looked like it was glassware straight from Wilma and Fred's dinner table.

'Aren't they beautiful?' Susan Castle added. 'The Cubist-inspired geometric forms make it one of the most original American glass designs of the 20th Century. It's the essence of Art Deco/Art Moderne.'

I flipped through the photos again without comment, because I hardly knew what to say. The stuff was absolutely horrid. It was unbelievably gross and though I collected Depression Glass and loved it all because it was so lovely and aesthetically pleasing, this stuff was quite different. The photos showed me items that were apparently pitchers, cups, plates, bowls and vases, all of various colours of glass, but hardly your garden variety, nicely-done Depression Glass. This stuff was composed of hard geometric shapes with harsh sharp angles that made each piece look twisted and bizarre. It was atrocious stuff.

I stared at each photo with astonishment and dismay, while the Castles spouted amazing monetary figures for the values of each piece. Five thousand, ten thousand, twenty thousand dollars for certain pieces. That the stuff was rare I could well believe, but that it was worth so much money seemed incredible.

'They're simple, yet so quintessentially Art Deco,' John Castle enthused. 'Rombic means irregular in shape with no parallel lines. Ruba came from Rubaiy, meaning an epic poem or perhaps it was a shortening of the designer, Ruben Haley's first name. No one knows for sure. It's not important. What is important is that our collection is gone and we want it back.'

'John and I bought each piece many years ago, Mr. Hollow,' Susan Castle added sadly.

'You can call me Ben, short for Bentley,' I said.

'Thank you, Mr. Hollow,' she replied ignoring my request. I could see she was devastated by the loss. She went on, 'We bought our pieces decades ago when there was no market to speak of, we paid very little. It was a steal, really. Since then however, advanced Art Deco collectors and even museums have started displaying Ruba Rombic. Prices have shot up astronomically.'

'Our problem, Mr. Hollow,' John Castle explained, 'is that we could never replace this collection if it were lost to us forever. It's not a matter of insurance money, it's that you cannot find the pieces anywhere. Period.'

'So they're scarce?' I asked.

'Rare, Mr. Hollow. They are rare, none are to be found,' Castle replied. 'It is estimated less than 1,500 pieces have survived.'

'So why me? Why not go to the police?'

John Castle nodded, 'Good question. We did go to the police, of course, initially. They told us . . . '

'Mr. Hollow,' Susan Castle interrupted, 'we know who took the pieces. It was Simon James, another collector.'

My eyebrows arched. I'd heard the name of course. James was a mover and shaker in our fair city.

'And you told this to the police?' I asked.

'Of course, but nothing was ever found in a search of James' home. James is a collector too, and has a wonderful grouping of pieces, among them a top-notch collection of Ruba Rombic, but of course all his pieces are validated with bills of sale from reputable dealers. He showed these to the detectives with obvious amusement. The police found nothing incriminating.'

'The bottom line, Mr. Hollow, is that our complaint, without any proof, means the police will not investigate any further. Captain Wallace told us he could not afford to bother such an important member of the community without conclusive proof,' Susan Castle said softly.

'Well, if what you say is true,' I said, 'he had to have a pro do the actual job. Someone from out of town, I'd guess. Tough to find. A man like James wouldn't steal it himself. But what makes you think a big shot like Simon James would do such a thing? And what would he do with this stuff once he had it? It's not the kind of thing he could easily sell. Even on the collector market, glassware like this would have a very limited interest. The other thing is, if James has a similar collection, why would he even want to steal yours? I mean, it doesn't make sense to me. And you say nothing else was stolen?'

'No, nothing else was touched, only our

Ruba Rombic,' John Castle admitted.

'I know that son-of-a-bitch stole my precious glass to . . . Well, you know what he's going to do with it, John? My God, I can't even say it!' Susan Castle's anger and hopelessness finally had gotten the better of her.

'Easy, Susan,' her husband said, comforting his wife with an affectionate hug. 'Why don't you go inside and lie down a while. I know you're upset. Take a pill and a nap. I'll square things with Mr. Hollow.'

Susan Castle dried her tears. 'Get them back for me, Mr. Hollow, please.'

I watched as she walked into a bedroom down the hall. There she shut the door behind her with a loud slam. I was left alone with her husband.

'My wife — she's emotional,' John Castle explained.

'I understand, but I don't know if I can help you. Honestly, this all sounds very confusing. Why would someone like Simon James steal this stuff?'

Castle sighed, 'He's a collector too, Mr. Hollow. He and I have the largest collections of Ruba Rombic in the world.

You see, Simon and I go way back, we began in business and politics decades ago, we also began buying up Depression glassware when it was dirt cheap — especially Ruba Rombic. Now each piece is going for big money.'

'Okay, I understand that,' I said, my eyes darting to the photos of the missing glassware. I shook my head wondering who would even want to collect this stuff. I figured the only reason it must be so valuable today is that when it was sold in the 1930s no one had bought it. I sighed, 'Look, what could a big-shot like Simon James do with the stuff? He could never sell it.'

'Mr. Hollow, my wife and I know Simon James well. He doesn't want to add our pieces to his collection. He doesn't even want to sell them for money. What Simon James wants to do with our Ruba Rombic collection — is destroy it. He will break each piece into tiny shards of useless glass. That is what is disturbing my wife so much.'

'But why destroy it?' I asked, amazed.

'So that he will have the best collection of Ruba Rombic in the world and so that his collection will increase substantially in value,' Castle said matter-of-factly.

I laughed, that certainly seemed twisted, but being a collector myself, I knew the collector mentality. Any collector worth his salt would never even consider such a thing, but a few — certain ones — well, they just might. I realized Castle's words were not as far from the realm of possibility as they sounded.

'And you and your wife actually believe this?'

'Years ago when we were on social terms, Simon even told us as much when he first saw our collection. He lamented how without the existence of our pieces, his own collection would become the finest in the entire world. He told me with a smile then how the value of his pieces would easily quadruple in value.'

I nodded, the dark side of the collector mentality.

'We can pay you well, Mr. Hollow,' John Castle continued, handing me a small piece of paper which I looked at, noting a substantial number followed by four zeroes. I gladly placed the cheque in my pocket.

Castle added, 'Can you look into it? See what you can find out? Please.'

'I'll look into it,' I said carefully, 'but I can't promise much if the police have come up empty. Any idea where James would stash the stolen goods?'

'No,' Castle said helplessly. 'The police didn't find anything incriminating at his home.'

'What about his destruction of the glass?' I asked. 'It's been a few weeks, it may be gone by now.'

Castle shook his head nervously. 'I hope not. I don't think so. He'd want to look each piece over, savour each item for a while before he destroys them. At least that's what I've told Susan, to calm her — she gets so worried that the glass may have already been destroyed.'

'And you don't think so?' I asked.

'No. Not yet. I don't think so.'

'I think you may be right, Mr. Castle,' I said, thinking of what I knew of the collector mentality — but I also knew I didn't have much time. I had a lot of work to do. I got ready to leave. 'I'll be in touch, Mr. Castle.'

John Castle's cheque would be a boon to my police pension and allow a bit left over to buy a Depression Glass piece I'd had my eye on in an Internet auction. Since my wife, Beth, had left me for a doctor last year, I'd been living alone in an empty house with only the glassware she had left behind for company. I missed the wife but at least I had the glassware. That Depression Glass really was quite lovely; bright, colourful, graceful even, with so many charming patterns — but this Ruba Rombic stuff . . . scheesh! I hadn't wanted to mention to the Castles that I thought the stuff was brutal. I mean, if my glass collection was made of vomit, I'd have Ruba Rombic too! Still and all, this was a paying case and I'd been given a nice-size cheque to do the job as best I could.

My first step was to call my friend Detective Jackie Harris to get the lowdown on just what the police file had on the robbery; also to get her take on the Castles and Simon James.

'Ben,' Jackie told me over the phone, 'a search warrant was issued and came up blank on the house on Michigan Avenue. As far as the robbery, it looked legit, but it's a dead end. No prints, the alarm was circumvented. The Castles were out of town at the time. Only that damn glassware was missing. It was a pro job for sure, or an inside job.'

'Inside job?' I asked quickly. 'What makes you say that?'

'Well, maybe. The husband and wife don't always seem to get along. There seems to be some tension there. That glass is supposed to be worth a small fortune, pretty amazing, eh? Anyway, my partner thinks that maybe one of them stole it, to hide it from the other?'

'Any evidence of that?' I asked.

'No,' she replied carefully. Did she know more than she was willing to tell me? I wondered. Usually Jackie was very up front, but now that I was retired and out of the loop, she might be holding back a card or two.

'I don't know,' I said thoughtfully. 'That doesn't make sense to me, from what I've just seen of them. They hired me together to find the stuff, they're both adamant that James stole it — or hired someone to steal it. And they do seem to get along well enough, your average retired older couple. I didn't see any tension between the two.'

'Oh well, that's all we have now. Nothing on the street about the break-in, or anything about any valuable glassware. We squeezed the usual fences and informants. Checked the local pawn shops. Nada.'

'What about Simon James?' I asked.

Jackie was silent for a moment, 'That's a bit complicated.'

'What do you mean?' I told Jackie the Castle's theory of why James had stolen their glassware.

'Yeah, I remember them telling us something like that. Seems crazy but I could see James being like that, you know, that kind of person. If he can't have it — no one else can.' Jackie said, then added, 'But, Ben, we've got nothing on him and he's got a lot of juice in this town. Captain Wallace was told to back off unless he had substantial and serious proof. Being Captain Wallace . . . well, you know.'

'Yeah, thanks, Jackie.'

Jackie's info didn't leave me much to go on. I made a mental note that I'd probably want to speak with Simon James at some point but in the meantime I did an extensive Internet search of the big man and this glassware. Not only Google, but I emailed all my contacts in the collectable glassware field for info. I wanted to know if James bought from them and what he bought. How did he pay? What was he like to deal with?

I came up with a lot of info, most of it seemingly contradictory. Simon James was a big player in the Depression Glassware field aside from being wealthy and powerful overall. He lived in a big house and collected all kinds of things but seemed to specialize in Art Deco works and Depression Era glassware. His house was filled with it — but it was big enough to hold whatever he wanted. By all accounts he had an extensive and priceless collection. It didn't make sense to me that such a man would cause this theft — unless you were a collector yourself and knew someone who was this type of collector, I kept telling myself.

I smiled, that's why John Castle had been so adamant on my taking this case, and why he knew that being a collector myself I was the right person for the job.

The Internet proved to be a wash. Contacts via email were better but didn't really pan out. James bought a lot of stuff from the same people and places I bought from — just a lot higher-end items for a lot more money. I was about to call it all off and close up shop on the Castles when I got a call from Jenny Rogers at Kalamazoo Arts.

'Hi, Ben,' Jenny said cheerily with her usual enthusiasm. We went back a bit, Beth and I had been buying and selling to her for years. I'd kept up the relationship. 'You know, you still owe me $75 for that Peach Lustre bowl.'

'Yeah, I remember, I was just going to send you a cheque,' I said. 'Don't worry, I didn't forget you.'

'I know, Ben. The cheque is in the mail.

I know you're busy and all. Look, I didn't call you to remind you to pay your bill — though that would be nice . . . '

I laughed, 'Sure.'

'And you didn't hear this from me, understand?'

'Yes,' I said, more attentive now.

'This Simon James; I've never met him but he buys from me a lot, also from some other dealers I know. Well, when you emailed me about what he buys and pays, it's only the best stuff and he pays top dollar. You can understand I don't want to lose him as a customer.'

'Sure,' I replied. 'I've heard all that. His house is full of only the best stuff. It's like a museum.'

'Well, that's just it. I ship almost all the stuff to his home on Michigan Avenue, but . . . '

'Almost? Where's the rest of the stuff go?'

'That's just it, he's got another house.'

'Really?' I asked totally interested now.

'Well, it's not really a house, it's some kind of hunting lodge up in the mountains. He's very secretive about it

213

and I always feel like I'm doing something not quite on the up-and-up when he has me ship there . . .'

I smiled, 'Jenny, you're a peach! What's the address?'

★ ★ ★

I drove up right away. The house was in the mountains outside of town. It was not exactly a hunting lodge and not exactly a mansion. I left my car on the side of the highway and walked up the icy road. The house was set back in the snowy woods, alone, quiet. It looked like it was closed for the winter. I wondered.

The place was a two-floor log home with a pointed roof and a wooden porch all around it. The lights were off. It looked deserted. I carefully walked up the pathway, onto the porch and found a doorbell. I rang it.

There was no answer.

I rang it again and again.

No answer again.

Now I had to decide, bite the bullet, earn my money for the Castles or give it up and slink away never to know the truth. I took a deep breath. B&E wasn't my usual thing but there were questions I wanted answered and besides, I needed the money. I used my shoulder to break in the front door. It wasn't a very solid door and after three tries it flew open and I staggered inside.

The place was dark, but there was enough daylight left for me to look around. What I found was an amazing accumulation of boxes — Postal Service, UPS, FedEx. Some opened, others still sealed. They were piled throughout every room; the place was overrun with various collectables. Especially glassware — Depression Era glassware. I walked around, marvelling at all the lovely objects, some things I knew I could never afford and would never own. I was amazed as I walked through room after room.

I found the Castles' Ruba Rombic collection on the kitchen table. All the missing pieces were there wrapped up in boxes. Now what to do?

I thought of calling the cops of course; making Simon James pay for his crime and even more so to me, his violation of the collector's code — stealing from a fellow collector. But it just didn't seem to make sense to get the cops involved and have them over-complicate everything. The cops would make a mess of it, asking *me* all kinds of nosy questions, with James eventually getting fancy lawyers involved. Those lawyers would make *me* the darn criminal. His people would accuse me of B&E, theft, whatever else they could. I knew that wouldn't end well for me.

Or, I could just put the stuff in my car and drive over to the Castles and give it back to them. Which is just what I did.

★ ★ ★

I carried the boxes into the house carefully, one at a time from the back of my car. The Castles were shocked and overjoyed when they looked at what was in those boxes.

'You found them!' Susan Castle cried in joy, suddenly planting a kiss on my cheek. She called her husband and they looked through each box in sheer delight.

'Mr. Hollow, you are amazing,' John Castle said obviously relieved. I placed the boxes on the dining room table and both husband and wife got busy going through each box, carefully unwrapping their precious objects, looking them over minutely, then lovingly placing them inside a large oak display case.

'John, they're home,' Susan Castle said in relief. She delicately placed the last piece of that infernally ugly Ruba Rombic into the display case and locked the glass door with a small key.

I smiled, 'I guess it's an acquired taste.'

'You either love 'em or you hate 'em,' John Castle answered with a knowing smile. 'So where did you find them? What did Simon James say when he was arrested?'

I held up my hands. 'There's not a lot to say about that. You wanted your precious Ruba Rombic back, so here it is. Safe and sound. The less said about any of this; my involvement, your suspicions about Simon James, or even the fact that you have it back at all — well, it would be best for all concerned to keep mum. You get my drift?'

'Then he gets away with it?' Susan Castle flared in anger.

'He gets away with nothing. Your property is returned to you and without any damage, just as you wanted,' I replied more forcefully.

She nodded slowly. I saw her face soften as she looked over at the rescued glassware that now filled her display case. 'Well, then thank you, Mr. Hollow . . . Ben. We won't say another word.'

'You did a hell of a job,' John Castle added. 'My only regret is missing out on seeing the look on Simon James' face when he realizes that the items he filched from us, have been filched from him. There's justice in that, at least. You've made my wife and I very happy. Thank you.'

'There's just one more thing, Ben,' the wife said rather hesitantly. 'This box over here. These six pieces. They are not ours.'

'Really? Are you sure?' I asked, watching as John now examined the pieces and soon concurred with his wife.

'Nope, not ours at all,' he stated.

'So what now?' I asked.

The Castle's looked at me, 'Well, they're not ours and we do not want them.'

'Well, I can't put them back now,' I stammered, perplexed by the problem. 'I mean, it was a big risk taking the stuff in the first place.'

'Well, why don't you just keep them? Susan Castle asked.

'Yeah, Mr. Hollow, Simon will miss them but then again, he probably stole them too,' John Castle added. 'Who knows, maybe you'll be contacted by the true owner and will be able to return them? If not, just look at it as the perks of the job.'

'I don't know, it would be too risky to return them now, and I guess I could hold on to them for a while . . . but that stuff is just . . . so damn ugly!' I said with a smile. Then I looked at the six pieces in the box more closely, 'You know, this stuff does kinda grow on you. I think I'm actually getting to like it. In fact, they might fit well in my own collection if no one claims them. After all, I am a Depression Glass collector and this Ruba Rombic is kind of unique.'